I0630843

NANCY E. POLIN

EVERNIGHT PUBLISHING ®

www.evernightpublishing.com

Copyright© 2019

Nancy E. Polin

Editor: CA Clauson

Cover Art: Jay Aheer

ISBN: 978-1-77339-902-7

ALL RIGHTS RESERVED

WARNING: The unauthorized reproduction or distribution of this copyrighted work is illegal. No part of this book may be used or reproduced electronically or in print without written permission, except in the case of brief quotations embodied in reviews.

This is a work of fiction. All names, characters, and places are fictitious. Any resemblance to actual events, locales, organizations, or persons, living or dead, is entirely coincidental.

NANCY E. POLIN

DEDICATION

For those who prefer to dream beyond themselves.

NANCY E. POLIN

GRAVE FORTUNE

Nancy E. Polin

Copyright © 2018

Prologue

Alexander Kelly took a swig of coffee more out of habit than any real desire. The action filled him with immediate regret when the cold bitter brew filled his mouth, barely avoiding his gag reflex.

He'd been driving for hours with no real destination in mind, agitation rubbing him from the inside out like sandpaper. A major decision had had to be made and he'd taken the step. He had nine more days with the Seattle PD and then he'd be moving on. The job prospect in Minneapolis had become a concrete offer late last week.

And his best friend was not happy about it.

Grimacing, he shoved the travel mug back in the cup holder and wiped his mouth with the back of his hand.

It didn't matter. He did what had to be done. He was leaving his home and everything he knew because he had no choice. He *had* to leave. Choice wasn't something he had the luxury of. He couldn't, he *wouldn't*, wreck things for Jesse.

Rolling his neck, Alex hoped to feel the release of tension in the popping of muscles. It didn't help.

He guided the truck over the darkened highway with familiar ease, eyes always moving, alert despite over 22 hours of wakefulness. He'd drop like a stone once his bed was in sight, but until then, instincts, coupled with his turmoil, kept him vigilant.

He turned onto a narrow road splitting from the main artery and maneuvered the truck up the winding incline, steering from memory as much as from what his headlights revealed. With the exception of college and four years in the army, he'd grown up in the area. The woods and surrounding mountains were his safe spot, and adulthood had yet to change the warm settling inside whenever he headed home.

Knowing he would be leaving it soon ate away at him.

Less than a half-mile from his driveway, the shoulder widened on the west side, leaving a long rutted area for turn arounds and parking for a handful of vehicles during hunting season. A couple of beater pickups and one SUV took up the normally deserted space and Alex frowned.

Big game season didn't kick in until fall. But then again, it could just be some folks roughing it for a couple of nights. If willing and able, a hike of about 7-10 miles could lead to camping with some spectacular views.

Alex's gut didn't line up with that possibility though.

He pulled behind the SUV. One bumper sticker proclaimed, "I'm hung like Einstein and as smart as a horse," while another warned, "Keep honking, I'm reloading."

Alex rolled down the window, cut the engine, and

listened for a moment. A brisk wind kicked up and sung through bristles of towering evergreens, but on the ebb, the faint sound of drunken guffaws reached him.

Definitely not the norm at 4:30 in the morning on a Monday.

His stomach seesawing, he reached across to pull his sidearm from the glovebox before grabbing his flashlight from the footwell behind the driver's seat. Climbing from the cab, he stepped lightly, securing his holster in an automatic motion. He swept the area with the low beam, following the partial footprints, narrowing his eyes at the sweep of marks in between. Unless his guess was off, these guys were dragging something.

All senses prickling to alert, Alex paused and debated calling it in. Hesitating, unease twisted low in his belly and a chill seeped into his blood.

If his hunch was correct, backup would be slow to react in a situation like this. It wasn't uncommon for many cops to not even bother. They looked at it as good riddance to something that shouldn't exist to begin with.

Anger bubbled inside and he pushed ahead to follow the narrowing path leading deeper into the woods. He wasn't a stupid man, so when it came to vampires, trust was not something attainable. At the same time, the creatures were still protected by law, much as humans were. Torturing or killing them was a felony.

On paper at least.

Of course, he could be completely off the mark, too. It remained to be seen. He doubted it, though.

He shoved through the foliage, careful not to twist an ankle in ground cover that pushed back against the trail. Despite the steady assent, Alex quickened his pace. Dark gray began to ease out the rich indigo of night. Dawn wasn't far off now.

Fifty or so yards further led to a small man-made

clearing and Alex paused at the edge to assess the situation.

Four men stood in a semi-circle around another who sat on the ground, hands tied behind him, securing him to the trunk of a storm-broken tree. His face hung forward, dark uncombed hair contrasting with the grey-toned skin.

Puzzled, Alex squinted at the scene.

He'd suspected what he'd find, but he hadn't expected to see a vampire so subdued. The creatures were strong enough to break through such modest bindings with ease, but this one didn't bother. Drugged maybe? Alex wasn't sure if that was even a possibility, didn't know enough about their metabolism to make that call. As he watched, the man turned his head just enough for Alex to catch the blacked-out eyes and sharp cheekbones of a starving vampire. The others hadn't noticed him, but Alex stood upwind. The creature could easily smell him and it dawned on Alex he hadn't taken any V-Guard over the weekend. He inwardly cursed. With any luck, two days off from the department's mandatory vampire protection wouldn't get him killed.

It didn't matter though. It had become too late for second thoughts the moment he pulled off the road.

The men stood around, drinks in hand, hips cocked to the side in snide indifference. One stepped forward to drizzle beer on the vampire's head and one of the others gave him a congratulatory slap on the shoulder and hooted. Two of the four held rifles and all of them looked barely old enough to shave.

There wasn't a whole lot of time. Dawn would soon light up the sky and the vamp would smolder and combust.

His badge clipped to his belt, Alex removed his handgun from its holster and stepped forward. The situation could take a sudden grave turn if the vamp decided to fight back. All four boys would be dead before they could contemplate the lack of wisdom in their actions.

And he'd be caught in the middle. Collateral damage.

Ignoring the tiny voice inside that firmly insisted he was a dumbfuck, Alex edged forward with his weapon out and announced his presence in a strong, clear voice.

All four boys froze, staring at him with wide eyes as he stepped from under the canopy. A moment later they all started babbling at once, voices high in denial and excuses.

"We were just—"

"He's okay. We didn't *do* anything—"

"Just goofing around..."

They all began to panic, gesturing at one another with broad strokes and Alex sighed.

"It was Bobby's idea. He said it wasn't no big deal. Said we'd just give 'im a little tan."

"Shut up, asshole!" His companion snarled at him, rubbing at the scruff of his cheek with the back of one hand.

The sky grew light a little too fast and Alex's gaze dropped to the vampire. It swung its head toward him but said nothing.

"All of you just shut the hell up!" Alex bellowed over the terrified finger-pointing. He could recite a laundry list of charges against them, but knew few would stick. Prejudice against vamps was rampant and few judges would "throw away a young man's future" over someone many argued wasn't even alive to begin with.

"Go home before I put you all so deep, you'll never see daylight again. *Now*."

They stared at him for only a moment, eyes wide

and bulging, before darting down the path Alex had just come up. One by one they brushed past him and he caught the smell of fear, beer, B.O., and cheap cologne. The sounds of branches thrashing and cracking carried back toward him, no doubt alerting every creature in the forest to stay clear. Engines without working mufflers vibrated through the night a few moments later.

Shoving his sidearm back into its holster, Alex pulled his pocketknife out and dropped to one knee by the vampire. Cool sweat rose against his brow. He knew the creature could smell his fear, but it didn't keep him from sawing through the twine that bound the man's wrists. "You fast enough to get to ground?"

"Doesn't matter."

"Are you serious?" Alex stared at him, but the vampire didn't look up.

"Just go before I take you with me."

"Well, man, that's not an option. At least not today." Pulling him up, Alex contemplated his direction for a few seconds before heading south. Another smaller path would shoot off from the clearing and if his memory wasn't faulty, there'd be a small cave to shelter the vampire for the day. It wouldn't be the most comfortable den, but he wouldn't turn into a coffee can's worth of ash either. "C'mon."

The vampire wasn't dead weight, but he didn't exactly help his cause either. Alex found himself sweating and swearing as he slung the creature's arm over his shoulders and dragged him from the clearing. Alex was a big guy. At 6'2" and 185 pounds, he kept in good condition, but the vampire wasn't all that much smaller than he was.

Night bled into day all around him, but the sun had yet to poke its way over the horizon. At best, he only had 10 or 15 minutes.

The path sprouted two others and Alex paused to remember. His brain fired frantically, hoping he hadn't misjudged his location. Breath rasping in his ears, he took an educated guess and continued on.

No, it was *this way.* He was sure of it. Over the years, the foliage must have just grown over the opening. It had to be just beyond the V of those two Spruce trees...

The vampire let out a low moan and folded forward.

Without thought, Alex stripped off his jacket, tossed it over the vamp's face and hunched to take the man's weight across his back in a fireman's hold. Stumbling when his foot caught in a surface root, he recovered his balance and pushed forward.

It had to be just a few more yards...

Around the next bend, Alex saw a crack of blackness against a steep incline. It veered just to the right. His muscles screamed as he asked more of them, stepping up his gait.

They'd both have to hunch over to enter, but the cave burrowed into the hillside deeply enough to keep the vampire safe until nightfall.

At the mouth, he dropped the man to his feet, grabbing him by the wrist as he did. Early morning sun sent its first tendrils of light and warmth siphoning through the woods and sudden intense pain knifed though his palm. Alex let go with a loud oath and gave the creature a hard shove forward before following him in.

Summoning what little energy he had left, he dragged the vampire to the very back wall, dropping him under a rock overhang. Dimly, he could smell the nauseating aroma of burnt flesh and wondered to what extent the damage was.

It didn't matter. He did what he could. He'd done his job. As far as he could tell, the vampire was still alive.

With one last glance at the man, he headed to the exit. Pausing, he gathered a few branches to hide the opening, gasping at the slice of pain in his hand.

Alex flipped it over, wincing as he inspected his blistered and oozing palm. He pulled a handkerchief from his pocket and gently wrapped the burn, knowing it could have been so much worse. With slow, careful steps, he hiked back to his truck.

****

Fifteen minutes later Alex pulled up his driveway and cut the engine in front of the garage. With a low groan, he rested his head against the steering wheel and relived the vampire rescue in fast-forward.

What the hell had he been thinking?

You know exactly what you were thinking. You can't seem to help yourself, you sanctimonious bastard.

Or was it something else? Had he been purposely reckless?

He recalled Jesse's face when a new realization dawned. *"It's not about a new opportunity is it, Alex?"*

The accusation burned him. Not that it wasn't true, but he couldn't figure what he could have said or done for Jesse to call him on it. Sure, he'd always been friendly to Dana, she was his best friend's wife after all, but what cue had shoved the truth out into the light?

He couldn't think for the life of him.

Not that it mattered now. He vaguely wondered if Jesse had said anything to her, but doubted it. What would even be the point?

With a heavy cleansing sigh, Alex stumbled from the truck and plodded up the path to his front door. The place was a modest design, courtesy of the 1950s, but its isolation and the back deck overlooking the creek made it a keeper. Of course, it had belonged to his parents, who sold it to him below market price when they decided to trade in the leaky faucet of the Northwest for the sun-filled dryness of Arizona. He couldn't imagine what they'd been thinking, but they'd never really seen eye to eye on that sort of thing. Now they seemed to appreciate golf courses in lieu of spiring evergreens.

He'd thought about selling the old place, but couldn't bring himself to do it. Renting it out was the only thing he could handle.

The aroma of paint and pine cleaner stung his nose as he let himself inside.

Great new weekend project he had for himself now.

Alex shook his head and, ignoring the growing stack of boxes, he stepped toward the galley kitchen his mom had always complained about. The kitchen window view of forest and creek had always stifled any real sting from her words.

Exhaustion clouded his eyes and exacerbated every single ache in his body, but he needed sustenance first. He also dimly registered the need to treat and dress his hand.

One thing at a time.

He gathered what he needed to make himself a sandwich and plopped down at the table. A cold beer tempted him, but he figured drinking at 6:00 in the morning was kind of messed up and settled with plain water.

A moment before his last bite, his cell phone buzzed to life in his pocket.

Yanking it out, he curled his lip, only to let it drop as a strange blankness washed over him.

Sam Cleary.

Why the hell would Jesse's father-in-law be calling him at six in the fucking morning?

Hesitating just a moment, he hit accept.

The man rambled in stops and starts, the flip side of his usual measured and articulate method of speaking. Horror and despair threaded his words together into a congealed mess and Alex felt everything inside grow cold.

Long after the call ended, he sat and stared through the small window above the sink, the slender fingers of early morning sunlight caressing the new growth of spring beyond.

In a sudden burst of emotional energy, he threw the phone against the wall, the screen shattering on impact before the expensive device smacked the floor.

He wasn't going anywhere.

Unless circumstances negated it, he had a promise to keep.

Chapter One

21 months later

Alex pulled in front of the pretty robin's egg blue bungalow and cut the engine of his truck. Dormant perennials awaited rebirth in the small front yard, while a few hardy winter flowers bloomed to pick up the slack. He didn't know one from another, but admired their courageous fight for life as temperatures snapped with frigid cold.

In some ways, they reminded him of the woman living within the walls of the little house. Seemingly delicate, but tougher than most would ever believe.

Hesitating, he peered up at the windows for a few more moments, aware she'd know he was out here with a knowledge that had nothing to do with a simple peek through the blinds. Anger he'd been trying to suppress threatened to bubble over and he took a long, cleansing breath.

He'd stopped calling her for this kind of thing. The toll it was taking on her had become much too apparent. The damn "gift" she'd been left with after the accident was slowly starting to eat her alive. Of course, Dana, being Dana, would never admit it.

Nope, he hadn't contacted her, but his captain had. That phone call had put him in an awkward position. She wouldn't say no, but at least Alex could be there for her and try to protect her the best he could.

With a low chest growl, he grabbed the evidence bag off the passenger seat and hopped out of the truck. A brisk wind pushed at his coat and tousled his hair, but he took another deep breath before stepping toward the bungalow, lava rock crunching under his boots.

Dana Chambers pulled the front door inward on his approach. Dressed casually in jeans and a flowing black tunic with some kind of beading around a V-neck, she had her dark chestnut hair pulled back from porcelain features into a single braid. When she offered him a genuine smile, something fluttered deep in his belly. Something not quite appropriate, considering their history.

"Hi. I thought you were going to sit out there and brood all night."

His own lips pulled to the side, answering her with the smirk he knew she'd anticipate. Climbing the few steps onto the porch, he felt the smile slide before he regained it. She looked good, her complexion peaches and cream, but he knew it wouldn't last. He'd watch the healthful glow bleed away tonight. "Nah, maybe next time though. Need to keep my hobbies honed ... *and* that came out sounding more than a little creepy."

The throaty silk of her laughter swept over him and he couldn't help but grin at her. Despite the circumstances, he could listen to it all day.

"I'm sure. Oh, gee. You even brought me a gift!" She teased when her gaze landed on the plastic bag in his hand.

Sobering, he said nothing, anger surging once more. He tamped it down to keep her from noticing. She stepped back, holding the door for him.

Alex followed her in, sweeping the interior with his gaze. "Hey, Bo."

The big shepherd/malamute mix sidled up to him for pets and he automatically scratched one shaggy ear. Tiny sounds of ecstasy escaped the dog's throat. There hadn't been a bark out of him. He knew Alex well.

Not much changed. Comfortable space, with warm hued walls, original wooden floors, area rugs matching the slightly oversized furniture. Photos lined the mantle of the fireplace and he didn't have to look close to know he was in a couple of them. Jesse's guitar still leaned in its rack in the corner behind the sofa and Alex had a quick flash of a last gathering of friends and family. "He shouldn't have called you. I'm sorry for that."

She studied him for a moment before waving him to take a seat. "Curt obviously thought this one was important."

They were always important. They always would be for a politician in training. A tidy record of putting criminals away would go a very long way.

Alex said nothing, keeping his thoughts and frustration to himself. She wouldn't take it well if he decided to be blunt. "Are you up to this tonight? Last time seemed a little rough."

She stared at him, her searching gaze steady on his. Her eyes were a rich, whiskey-brown and depending on the light, he could sometimes see gold flecks within. He thought she might be attempting to read more into his observation, but he'd kept his tone conversational.

After a moment, those beautiful eyes warmed and she shrugged. "Some are harder and that's all it is. I get home afterward, drink some orange juice, grab some sleep and then I'm good as new." Her words hastened toward the end of her reassurance and she dropped her gaze. Reaching out, she stroked her dog as the animal rested his muzzle on her knee.

A strong sense of foreboding settled inside, weighing him down. He didn't like being lied to and felt that's what she'd just done. Or at least she'd lied by omission. It didn't matter though. He knew if he opened his big mouth, she'd just shove right back. He wondered what her late husband would think of all this. Although he'd been gone for almost two years, Alex could easily foretell his best friend's reaction. He'd be pissed off. He'd resent Dana allowing herself to be used this way. Of course, naturally, she didn't see it in that light. She saw it as some kind of masochistic call of duty.

Dana wasn't the only one with a masochistic streak. Even now he wondered why he did it to himself. If he were smart, he'd be looking for another opportunity. That place in Minneapolis had wanted him and he knew damn well there would be others just like it.

But he also knew deep in his flesh, muscles, and bone that he could never leave.

Without another word, she held out her hand. "I presume everything's set?"

Alex nodded. He had uniforms and plain-clothed on standby. Some had been through the routine before and allowed her a certain awed respect, while others would watch her like she was some kind of circus curiosity. Occasionally, a cop would wear their animosity right near their badge. Her reputation brought a mixed bag of reactions. Still, he hesitated.

She frowned, reading his reluctance. "C'mon, Alex. Hand it here."

He inwardly sighed and held the bag out to her.

Her fingers curled against the plastic and her face tensed. Blood stained the T shirt. Not much, just a fine spray. He knew she wouldn't ask. She never did. As far as he understood, her talent didn't fill in those gaps, and he was thankful for that. Dana broke the seal, reached in to brush the fabric with her fingertips and jolted.

Bokken barked in alarm and Alex pushed to his feet, but when she just shook her head, he lowered himself back into the cushions. Tension rippled through him and the muscles at the back of his neck bunched, but he willed himself still.

She touched the cotton again, careful to avoid the dried blood. Her brows pulled together, tiny lines creasing the flesh for several moments before her face went lax, eyes sliding into the eerie blankness he'd come to despise.

Dew drops of perspiration broke through her flesh and her breathing went choppy. A violent tremor vibrated through her and Alex cursed softly under his breath.

"So young. Such a dark aura," Dana murmured. "Black soul. Nothing left."

She was right. The man they hunted tonight was barely out of his teens.

Her knuckles whitened as she clung to the fabric, some inner electrical connection holding tight. "Still here. Close. Hiding. Scared, but angry. So much rage."

When she rose, her expression didn't change. She seemed unaware of the movement, but Alex followed, noting her slight limp with a frown. Had it been there when he'd first arrived? *So many painful souvenirs from the accident.*

He grabbed her coat from the rack by the door and gently placing it over her shoulders, made sure to lock up behind them.

****

There was a time early on when his reaction to her gift had been dubious. How could it not be? But she'd threatened to go on her own. He'd tagged along and now knew that night had opened Pandora's Box. Worried, he weighed calling it quits tonight. It was doubtful she'd even have the energy to complain. She huddled in the passenger seat of his truck, a small fine-boned woman who could pass for a teenager. But not now. The hunt aged her. Her face gaunt, pale, her eyes hollowed out. No one could ever mistake her for a healthy woman.

"The turn's coming up soon, Alex."

Hating himself, he'd followed her quiet direction into a part of South Seattle that still offered somewhat affordable real estate at the expense of drug deals, prostitution, and the occasional murder. Many formerly beautiful homes now sat forlorn and in need of a caring touch, with the exception of the occasional scrappy senior citizen who'd planted their heels during the glory days and had no intention of ever moving.

"Okay." Through his ear piece, he noted the restlessness of his men. Shuffling, gum cracking, the occasional dirty joke.

"Next left." She pressed her lips together and grimaced. "No, wait. One after that."

"Maybe we should have had her sniff Hayes's boxer shorts." A gravelly voice broke out from the background noise just as another told him to shut the fuck up. Alex approved of the reprimand. It saved him the trouble.

"About a half block, on left," Dana murmured, eyes closed, forehead creased in concentration and pain. "He's agitated, jumpy. Watchful."

"What have we got?" Another voice called out. Alex flinched at the sudden crackle in his ear accompanying it.

"Small one-story ranch, set back from the street, two front windows, probable basement, porch light off, but lights on in front room. Empty lot north, can't tell what's behind. And my grandmother's house is just south of it."

"*What*?"

"Kidding. Just looks like my grandma's house with flowers, a donkey cart and those creepy lawn gnomes. That kind of stuff. No activity from what I can see. Grandma and Grandpa probably went to bed."

"You know what to do." Alex broke through the banter, bringing everyone to ready.

Chapter Two

One van passed him and continued toward the house in question, stopping at the next block, lights off, engine running. Two more unmarked followed suit. Others spread out to net the area.

Broken streetlights allowed winter darkness to press down upon them. Shadows of towering firs flickered when clouds thinned and exposed the moon, only to congeal once again. The neighborhood remained quiet, but Alex knew it could shift too quickly.

"Anything else we need to know, Dana?" Alex peered into the woman's face, uneasy at her pinched expression.

"Yeah, like are there any vamps in there? That would be a good thing to know, ya think?" The gravelly voice blared in his ear again. "Those fuckers are formidable."

"Hell, you have nothing to worry about. You probably took twice the dose of *guard*. You even smell bad to *me*." Another voice broke through, guffaws following.

"Nah, man, he always reeks like that. That's how pussies smell."

More boisterous laughter crackled in his ear and Alex winced.

"Of course I took my dose. Being cautious doesn't make me a pussy." The man sounded defensive, sulky, but in the face of fellow cops, it quickly turned to bravado. "My mom and dad only raised one idiot and that one's my kid brother."

"Sure it is."

"Shut up."

"Okay guys, knock it off. There's no evidence he associates with vampires." Alex sighed against the banter. Many cops automatically lumped crime with vampires, but in Alex's experience, most of the time it wasn't the case. More often than not, the creatures kept to themselves, shunning the general populace. Nonetheless, as a precaution, procedure dictated every cop take a dose of department issued *V-guard* before going on duty. "Roy? How's that warrant coming? Who we got tonight?"

His partner's voice cut through the nervous chatter. "Judge Kramer's up."

Alex nodded out of habit, despite knowing Roy didn't have a visual on him. Relief paraded through him on little cat paws. Kramer had stood in their corner before. Some judges were a lot more skeptical.

She hadn't responded to his question and Alex's worry heightened. Dampness broke against his brow despite the cool temperature. "Dana? Anything else we need to know?"

Her dark eyes flew open, expression anguished. Her hands shot out and grabbed his arm, fingers pressing in. She was stronger than she looked. "Alex, there's an innocent."

Shit.

"Can you separate it?"

"Innocent? LT, what does that mean?" A separate, younger voice filled his head. The rookie.

"Most likely a kid, although a compromised adult is possible." Alex responded, steady gaze still on the woman beside him.

"It's away from the others. Back room. So soft. Probably a sleeping child." A moment passed before Dana met his eyes. Hers were filled with terror and dread. "His darkness is overwhelming. Two others are with him, beside the little one. He could snap. You have to be careful. Please."

"Okay." He squeezed her shoulder with a gentle hand. "It's time to get you the hell outta here."

Roy's voice filled his head. "Alex, we have the warrant."

****

Somewhere between White Center and the freeway entrance leading north, Dana lost some time. During the effort of the hunt, her head threatened an implosion, so unconsciousness was a sweet relief. The blackness offered no worries, no pain and no memories. Sometimes she wondered what it would be like to escape permanently, just let the darkness rise over her and pull her into its depths.

"Ms. Chambers?"

Someone caught her arm and shook it. She wanted him to stop and let her continue to ride the peace of the tides. He persisted and she managed an irritated grunt.

"Ms. Chambers!" The voice sharpened and the grip on her arm tightened into borderline painful.

When her eyelids fluttered apart, the worried face of a young man hung over her. His blue-gray eyes were huge and fearful. *Oh, that's right.* This was the rookie Alex had had bring her home the last few times.

"I'm okay." Her voice sounded hoarse and far away. She cleared her throat and tried again. "Really, I'm fine."

He frowned, dark lines cutting into his youth, adding a few extra years before her eyes. "Maybe I should take you to the hospital."

"No." She shook her head, a little dizzy at the action.

"The LT is going to kick my ass—"

"No. He's *not.*" She blinked the currents of darkness away. "There's no reason. Look, I'll get some rest and it'll all be good."

Frowning, he eyed her. "No offense, Ms. Chambers, but it seems worse, somehow, this time. Are you sure you shouldn't get checked out? Just to be safe?"

"I'm fine. Don't worry about the Lieutenant. I can handle him." She hoped. Each hunt it got much more difficult to shrug off his worries. It alternately touched and annoyed her.

Torn, he continued to watch her for a few long moments before giving a curt nod. "I'll walk you up though. Just so you know, if the LT kills me, I'm gonna come back and haunt you."

A smile twitched at the corner of her mouth. "Fair enough."

She let Davey—*his name was Davey, right?*—take her arm and help her from the car. Dana knew Alex had a reputation of being overprotective of her, and the kid's fears were far from unwarranted. Alex just didn't need to know *everything.*

Dana gently pulled from his grasp, pausing to squeeze his arm in gratitude. Her body trembled, but cool droplets of fog coated her face, helping to soothe the thumping in her head. She sucked several full breaths in, savoring the metallic sweetness of impending rain and trying to shake away all the worries battling for dominance.

He followed her up the short path toward home, shadowing a little too close for her taste. She climbed the few brick steps leading to her front door and pulled her key ring from the pocket of her coat. The kid's loyalty to Alex was admirable, but she needed space now. Well, as much as she ever got.

She tried not to consider Alex's growing level of

discomfort. Things were getting harder for her, she couldn't deny it, but his adamancy that she stop came from somewhere else. She just wasn't sure how to handle it.

Unlocking the deadbolts, she used her shoulder to push the heavy door open and stepped into the comforting warmth of her entry, taking a moment to disarm her security system. Bokken greeted her with happy little whines and pushed at her hand. He wriggled with pleasure when she scratched him. "Hey Bo, how's my boy?"

While the big dog smiled his canine smile up at her, she turned to the young man eyeing the animal with a trace of wariness. Bokken knew him as a friend and unless the boy did something stupid, that wouldn't change.

"Thanks, Dave, I'm think I'm good."

"No problem. Don't forget to lock up." He continued to watch the 82-pound dog.

"Will do." Dana didn't hear the clunking of his boots on her front steps until she'd thrown the last deadbolt. She sighed when the roar of the police car's engine met her ears.

"Bo, you need to pee?" Dana looked down at the dog who never failed to leave her side when she was home.

He swished his tail and pushed his cold nose into the palm of her hand.

"All right then. It's been a tough night, so no fooling around, okay?" She crossed through the kitchen, unlocked the back door and swung it outward so the dog could take care of business. The chill flowed over her and she shivered, while Bokken wandered the yard, hitting both the Hemlock and the Douglas fir. After sniffing for a few more minutes, he returned to her, liquid tawny eyes staring up at her.

"Done?"

The dog continued to stare.

"Sure?"

Bokken gave a hardy sneeze and stepped past her into the house.

Shrugging from her coat, she hung it on the freestanding rack near the back door. Dana took a moment to recheck all locks and her security before turning out every light but one and heading upstairs. The dog followed her, staying at her left heel.

Muscles tense and trembling, head still aching from the evening's effort and her ambivalence concerning Alex, she barely had time to strip off her clothing, pull on pajamas, and curl up on her side of the bed. Sleep swallowed her instantly.

Hesitating only a moment, Bokken left his huge dog bed under the window, jumped on the mattress next to Dana and dozed with his big head resting on her hip.

Chapter Three

Exhaustion sank into every inch of his body, but his muscles coiled and burned as if expecting the night to just begin. It always took him a while to come back down during the aftermath of a hunt and now it was even worse.

Alex rolled his neck and shoulders to relax his upper body, but his anxiety dug in harder, culminating into throbbing pain at the base of his skull.

Choosing to avoid construction on I-90 on the Seattle side, he gritted his teeth as he drove north to catch 520 across the lake. It was more than just tension. Anger flared in waves through his bloodstream. He wasn't even sure why he was so angry, other than Dana's continual relaxed ability to dismiss her pain and discomfort. To see her in that condition tore a jagged hole inside, made worse by the press of guilt.

Despite the late hour, he'd almost driven back to Dana's place, stopping only by sheer force of will. He'd been ready to unload all his frustration, worry, anger, and fear, but some tiny, yet logical part of his brain warned against it. At least for now.

They'd done some good tonight. There was no denying it. Dana's instincts were correct, as always, and they'd been able to subdue the gunman. Aside from some minor cuts and bruises, the hostages were safe, including the child in the back bedroom. To no small degree, that's what perpetuated her behavior. It helped fill a void inside Dana, that gaping emptiness that exploded into existence when Jesse was sadistically replaced by her talent. Or curse.

Jess, I'm sorry. I didn't mean for this to happen.

But then he wondered why he *should* feel guilty. All this wasn't his doing. He'd kept an eye on her, just like he'd promised over that drunken game of pool all those years ago. At the time he hadn't taken it seriously, probably neither one of them had, but Jesse had grabbed his arm in one lucid moment within a series of besotted ones.

"If something happens to me, you'll look after her, right?"

"Sure man, whatever you want."

An intense light beamed in Jesse's eyes. "I mean it, Alex. She's everything to me. I need you to promise."

"Okay, okay. I promise."

A moment later, Jesse released him, aimed his cue stick and bounced a striped ball off the bar, missing a burly dockworker by about four inches. He hadn't brought it up again, but despite his own inebriation at the time, Alex hadn't forgotten.

Of course, that was long before he'd realized his own feelings had ... evolved.

He shook his head, trying to dislodge extraneous thoughts to concentrate on his driving.

A steady rain and wind brought choppiness to the surface of the lake, but not enough to swell water onto the floating bridge. There had been many times in the past when waves crashed up and almost over old 520, while he'd made the trek over Lake Washington to the Eastside. The memories never ceased to unnerve him. Although the new bridge traversed the lake at a higher elevation, the idea of a couple hundred feet of watery void below him filled with the wrecks of aircrafts, boats, all manner of garbage and God knew what else, was not something he cared to contemplate, preferring to sequester the knowledge to some unused corner of his brain.

The freeway connected to land once more and he guided his SUV toward 405 to drive south to pick up 90 east and home. He exited, but, changing his mind, made a U-turn to jump back on the freeway and go to the 24-hour gym instead. He was too keyed up and frustrated to go home alone and sleep. He had a hanging bag in his garage, but he wanted bright lights and free weights. With any luck, an intense workout would sap his strength and whitewash his mind.

He pulled into the parking lot, cut the engine and sat for a few moments to scan his surroundings. Floor to ceiling windows normally showcased dozens of the vain after a typical 9 to 5, but at two in the morning, no one flexed and sweated for the masses. He would have preferred a much more subdued place to work out, but with his erratic hours, he had to take what he could get.

Alex grabbed his duffel bag from the back seat. The echo of his truck door bounced against the macadam and reverberated through the fog rolling in around him, but something in the air made him pause. Prickles itched the back of his neck and he turned slowly, eyes roaming.

The figure made its way from the adjacent sidewalk and across the parking lot. He slouched, fists jammed in the pockets of an old sweatshirt, stopping when he noted Alex's heavy gaze. It was a boy, maybe 19 or 20 in appearance, but the slow knowing smile could mean one of two things—either he'd experienced sunrises and sunsets before Alex's first breath or he embraced the cockiness of a newbie. There was no way to be sure either way.

A stirring of fear rose in his blood and he tried to clamp it down. The creature would know, as much an animal of senses as of scents. Alex stood still, waiting and holding his breath. Just because most avoided humans, didn't mean all of them did.

The man stepped closer. "Have a cigarette?"

"No, sorry. Quit a couple of years ago."

"That's a shame. It's good for quieting the nerves." His smile returned and through his peripheral vision, Alex could see darkness flooding the man's eyes. Not a good sign.

Maybe he wasn't as old as Alex worried. Fledglings were often more brazen, if not outright stupid. That's probably why there weren't many of them. "Eh, it always made me a little jumpy. That and the whole lung cancer, emphysema possibilities. I tend to think quitting was one of my better decisions."

When the breeze shifted, the vampire started and took a half step back. He angled his head back, sniffing and wrinkling his nose. "What the hell *is* that?"

Alex said nothing and just watched. If he tried to run, the thing could be on him in an instant, but it didn't appear he needed to worry about it. His dose of *V-guard* should have been wearing off, but apparently there was enough in his system to smell distasteful to this one.

Hesitating, confusion rippled over his young features. "Is that *you*?"

"Probably. Sorry about that. Stressful night and didn't hit the shower yet. Looks like you might have to look elsewhere for your midnight snack, sparky. Think something four-footed. Most of your big brothers and sisters don't like rocking the boat."

The boy hissed and a trickling of sweat slid down between Alex's shoulder blades. *Nice one, Kelly. If he's a rogue, poking and taunting would not be considered the best course of action. V-guard or not, the vampire could rip him to shreds before he could even blink. It was a deterrent, usually a successful one, but not always.*

"You smell like shit." With that parting shot, the kid stepped around him, crossing the parking lot. He headed toward the 24-hour supermarket and Alex watched, muscles tense, vigilant despite the thrash of his heart.

Tired or not, his instincts pulled at him. Something felt *off*. Maybe his night wasn't over after all.

Moving faster than the human eye, the young vampire disappeared and reappeared just before entering through the sliding doors.

Why the hell would a vampire need to venture into a grocery store?

Alex dropped his gym bag and followed at a trot. The fog enveloped him, amplifying the sound of his boots against the macadam. He reached for his sidearm, knowing it wouldn't kill the creature, but aware it might slow him down a bit. The thought of calling for backup filtered in but dissipated. There was nothing to report. Instincts didn't count.

He increased his speed to a run, turning sideways as he entered the store.

The vampire spoke with one of the cashiers, a pretty young girl with blonde hair pulled into a ponytail and the tan of a salon bed. Her expression read annoyance before her eyes bugged and she blanched. Shaking her head, she tried to walk away before the creature caught her by the arm, fingers digging in. Pain and terror radiated over her features and her mouth drooped open. Tears filled her eyes. "Don't, Randy. Please."

Alex took a step forward, weapon rising. "You need to let her go. Now."

The boy smiled, his fangs catching the light and gleaming. "What you going to do with that piece of shit? Fuck off."

At the same moment two figures flanked before passing him to approach the young vampire. One of them, a tall flaxen-haired male, looked over, caught his eye for the briefest of moments and allowed a slow nod.

Fear crawled around inside, a natural response to a superior predator and Alex stopped. This would not be his fight. From his limited understanding, they often took care of their own. He wondered how long this particular creature had been a problem for its brethren.

The few people clustered at the front of the store backed away when the two vampires approached the first. He released the girl, but bared his teeth in defiance. It was an unwise choice. The tallest of the three snagged him by the throat and a deep growl drowned out the adult contemporary music piping through the ceiling speakers.

Alex felt the blow a moment later when he was knocked sideways. They'd brushed past and pushed him aside much as an unthinking adult might a child. Although he hadn't seen the movement, he managed to catch himself against the edge of the door at the last minute to keep from going down.

The next instant, an agonized scream knifed through the air, cut off abruptly before it could be absorbed by the fog. Apparently, justice didn't lag in the vampire world.

Heart ramming against his ribs, Alex searched the darkness more out of habit than expectation. Exhaling in a sudden gust, he replaced his weapon. Massaging his shoulder, he was vaguely surprised it hadn't been broken or dislocated.

No gym tonight. Screw it. He was *done*.

Chapter Four

Dana's eyes popped open and for a long, agonizing moment, she expected to hear the steady beeping and whirring of machines, feel the tubes and needles and unrelenting pain snaking through her body. She expected the confusion, the blurry helplessness of a coma patient. She expected the sting of alcohol and disinfectant in her nose.

When all she saw were familiar shapes huddled within the darkness of her own bedroom, she allowed the slow release of pent up breath to hiss from between dry lips. Her relief felt tangible, alive and tingling, but to her annoyance, her body continued to shake.

The nightmare never changed.

****

Jesse sighs and that troubled light shines in his pale blue-grey eyes when he glances over. He's disappointed, but there's low level anger simmering through that she still didn't understand. She only knew, or sensed, it wasn't directed at her.

She reaches over to squeeze his hand, lacing their fingers, trying to give him comfort. His hand is so much bigger than hers, but it's warm and gentle. His thumb slides over her wedding ring, an automatic, loving gesture to the testament of their six years of marriage. They'd married young, but it was true. She knows he'll eventually open up to her. Jesse is always the type to mull over a problem for a day or two, but he'd then sit down to share his thoughts with her. He'd ask her advice.

The next moment those high beams cut through the windshield to shock her eyes and blind her. Breaking contact, Jesse pulls his fingers free to grip the steering wheel, to right a wrong or maybe avoid one. The screech of metal against metal slices the night and they go into a sickening spin, bouncing several times against concrete. Dana jerks forward, backward and from side to side, not unlike a dog's favorite toy. She is held in place by the belt that steals her breath, but keeps her in her seat. She can't scream. It doesn't come. Not yet. Something new and unforgiving hits her from the right, the numbness immediate and terrifying. Pain engulfs her seconds later when shocked nerves snap into cruel awareness. The car is propelled into motion a second time, but she's too dizzy to figure which direction or where they might stop. She can't think if they'd cleared the bridge or if they'd somehow break through the barrier and sink into the vastness of the lake. The prospect sends pure white panic through her body and into her soul.

Round and round they go, where they stop nobody knows…

When the car finally comes to rest, she opens her eyes to gaze at the passenger window smashed into ornate spider webbing. She takes note of the crimson stains and rivulets and how they run into a prism with an almost calm puzzlement. It's actually kind of pretty. And the car isn't sinking. Relief is there, but it takes up so little of her.

Words don't come. They can't form. There seems to be some disconnect between her brain, vocal cords, tongue, and teeth. Or maybe they're lost in the fiery blaze of pain and torment. She starts to realize she can't figure where it begins or where it ends. Maybe it doesn't end and won't. The sickly sweet-pungent scent of blood is heavy in the air. Her body is broken. With deliberate care, she moves her head. Okay, maybe not everything is broken, but God, how she hurts. The pain swells and any light narrows into a pin prick before it widens into a shimmering chasm. Her brain must be dented and is now beyond repair. But she's still conscious and also stubborn. Her husband, father, and brother never passed up an opportunity to remind her of this less than sterling trait. She didn't care and still doesn't.

Despite her body's protests and her primal mind's attempt to protect her ... *don't look, don't look, don't look* ... she carefully swivels her head to look over at her husband.

Even then, she doesn't find words. Only hoarse, anguished screams propelling her into a long-ago darkness.

And those screams always followed her into the current waking world.

****

God, how many times had she recounted it to that therapist? She was fairly certain she'd lost count before she cut him off. Of course, he'd balked. She was a curiosity after all. Not many people bring their own dark talisman back from a coma with them as a continuous reminder to what they've lost. Or what they'd become.

Pushing the comforter back, Dana kicked free, absently pulling at the tank top she'd slept in where it clung to her, sticky with sweat. She glanced at the clock, unsurprised when 12:34 glowed back at her in red.

The exact moment of impact.

Bokken whined and hopped down off the bed. The big dog stretched, giving her the side eye.

"It's okay. I'm okay," She murmured, resting a hand on his broad head.

The headache blanketed her eyes, sharpening in the right temple as it always did. Rubbing it with two fingers, she padded to the bathroom to run cool water. She didn't bother with the overhead. The small nightlight she'd left burning was more than enough to see the reflection of the haggard ghoul currently posing as a person. Caverns swallowed her eyes and dented her cheeks. Her skin was waxen, lips bloodless, hair damp and limp. Most of the time she passed for a young, attractive woman. But when the nightmare came, that small comfort was always stolen from her.

Dana pressed chilled water against her heated face, half expecting steam to rise from her skin. The headache continued to thump behind her eyes, rising to a crescendo in that one little corner. She dimly wondered if she should delve into her personal pharmacy of over-the-counter and prescription medication, unsure where this one might land on her personal Richter scale. Or maybe she'd shun the meds all together and hope her body knocked it out before it could take over and put her on her back. At one time she *could* fight them off, but it hadn't happened in quite a while.

No. She couldn't take the chance. She had too much work to do later in the morning and couldn't risk it. One of her clients wanted their doggie daycare site up and running by week's end and she had several other designs to work on. She needed sleep, not torment.

She wandered downstairs, gripping the bannister, the pain setting her a little off-balance. Her right leg and hip ached in conjunction with her head and she allowed an inner sigh. *Never rains but when it pours.* Bokken followed dutifully. Her canine protector and shadow. Dana would have smiled if it didn't hurt so much.

By the subdued lighting of a single sconce off the kitchen and the overhead above the range, she put on the kettle, figuring tea, a painkiller and more sleep might chase the physical and psychological ache away. As she scooped tea into the infuser, she dimly wondered if Alex was awake. Possibly. He may still be tied up with last night's hunt. She expected she'd hear from him later in the day.

Taking her tea, she carried it to the bar separating the kitchen from the dining room and slid onto one of the stools. The parade of medication stood within easy reach. Most she needed to keep her brain in line, at least that's how'd she'd come to think of it. Some was 'as needed.' She took one of the latter and washed it down with her tea.

Of course no drug could suppress the other thing. It was always there, either on the periphery or forefront. She'd been able to put the dark talisman to work for the police, figuring if she was forced to carry the burden, it may as well allow her to do something productive.

But sometimes, it flooded out unbidden to overwhelm and suffocate her.

Like now.

Dark tendrils slid into and over her brain and a low moan escaped before she could bite it back. Dana pushed up from the stool, leaning against the bar. Her dining room and living room spread before her, the front door at the far side. There was no sound from inside or out, but she knew someone stood beyond her home, beyond her windows with their closed blinds and pulled curtains.

The aura felt black and sickening, heavy, oily. It was born of an older, experienced mind. One who'd committed heinous acts.

A low rumbling filled the room and some part of her recognized Bokken's response to the perceived threat outside. The sound left no debate the dog meant business. Anyone attempting to enter the house would be hurt.

Her dog and top of the line security should have made her feel better, but emotions and instincts always trumped pragmatism. Her heartrate bolted and sweat popped out against her suddenly chilled skin. Trembling that had ceased during the familiar tea making ritual, swung back over her, making her limbs weak and her teeth chatter. Nausea seesawed in her belly and she pressed a hand there.

Only dark diseased auras affected her this way. She'd just gone through it last night.

Whoever you are, please go away.

Dana fumbled against the bar and grabbed for her phone, knocking over pill bottles in her haste. Avoiding the center of the room, she inched sideways toward the front window, trying to make herself even smaller than her slim 5'4" frame.

The person outside hadn't moved closer, but they hadn't gone away either.

Bokken's growl graduated from throat to chest and he pressed against the side of her leg.

Gulping air, she made herself slow down, afraid she might hyperventilate. Her fingers tightened around the phone, a layer of sweat separating flesh from plastic. She switched hands, wiping her palm down her pajama bottoms.

It would be easy enough to call 911. Alex had a car pass by numerous times during the night and the uniform could be on her doorstep in seconds.

And tell them what? *Yeah, there's this dark aura hanging outside my secured house and I'm fearful for my safety.*

No, tell them you have an intruder on your property.

It's not close enough to be on my property.

Lie, you idiot.

She shook her head, biting back a cry when pain surged.

Gritting her teeth, she reached to push the curtain back a bare inch. Just enough to take a peek between blinds. The street was dim, the closest lamp a half-block south. Dana narrowed her eyes, heart twisting at the figure across the street. He wasn't close enough to set off the motion detector lights, so she could only make out a long coat and dark hair. His face was lost to the shadows, but there was nothing intimidating about his stance. He seemed almost casual, even rocking on his heels as she watched. But the black cloud emanating from him clogged her breath and fuzzed her mind. The thump of her headache hadn't been snuffed out by the painkiller yet, so dots danced before her eyes. Blinking them away, she pulled in one ragged breath after another before remembered the phone in her hand.

Alex. She should just go ahead and call him. He'd understand. He was the only one who did. Even her own father had a hard time with it.

Don't be stupid. Look, the guy's leaving.

Such a powerful aura. Pressing in, stealing her oxygen, and little strength she had … shutting her down … oh, God…

She pushed back, biting her lip hard and drawing blood. The new, sharp pain helped her focus.

The man shook himself off, as if he'd been daydreaming all along and turned to head toward a sleek dark sedan parked in front of her next-door neighbor's home. The license plate was obscured by Mrs. Bittle's love affair with hedges and he then drove from view in seconds.

Allowing the drape to fall back into place, Dana's legs gave out and she crumpled to the smooth wooden floor.

Chapter Five

Dana settled in the small office she once shared with Jesse, coffee in hand.

His side hadn't changed, walls covered with all manner of martial arts weapons. He'd been proficient in several techniques and had spent several hours a week training at a local dojo. Not that it had mattered in the end. Physical fitness and taut muscles were no match for a big rig with a sleepy driver.

She tried to concentrate on her work, but lack of rest the night before had her concentration wavering and blurring.

Two dark auras within hours of one another had taken their toll on her. There was little wonder she'd awakened on the floor with a big dog licking her face. At least, from as far as she could tell, she hadn't been out long. The presence outside had been gone and she'd had no desire to track it.

Dana stared at the screen and listened to the rain smack against the heavy leaded glass of her windowpanes. The storm had kicked in early that morning, but she'd always enjoyed the sound and smell of them. Too many people claimed the overcast skies depressed them, but it had never bothered her. She found comfort in it.

Pressing the heels of her hands against her eyes, she watched the light show explode behind them. Exhausted in mind and body, sleep had remained slippery and teasing the rest of the night. Now that she really needed to be alert, her rest deficit came back to haunt her.

She took a swallow of her coffee, unsure if the

caffeine would even do anything at this point.

The sudden rapping at the front door had her jumping and almost spilling the hot liquid in her lap. With a muttered curse, she put the mug aside and lurched to her feet.

Bokken hadn't barked and Dana knew why. She hadn't been looking for it, but she could now feel the presence outside just as much as her dog could sense it. Warmth slid over her.

Alex.

Usually he called first, so the unexpected visit sparked a trip in her heartrate as unease crept within to shrug aside the initial pleasure.

Or was it something else?

Dana pressed her lips together as she made her way downstairs. She kept a hand on the bannister just in cast her hip decided to clench up.

She wasn't stupid, nor was she naïve.

Things had started to shift and she didn't know how to deal with it. *There.* She acknowledged it. Pausing to blink up at the ceiling, it made no difference.

Of course, acknowledgement didn't make it any better. The situation was too emotional. Too damned *complex.*

Wasn't it?

Her thoughts and emotions felt like a direct betrayal to her husband, but, at the same time, it wasn't fair. Jesse was gone. The accident that had put her in a coma for over a week had taken him away from her in an instant.

But, God, how she'd missed him. She still did. He'd been a huge part of her life since her freshman year in college. Since he'd wandered into their shared elective, Native Art of the Pacific Northwest. The class had been interesting, but not as interesting as Jesse. He'd been smart, funny, sweet, compassionate, but with a steel backbone when merited. He'd also been her best friend for close to a decade.

And now he was gone and Alex had slid into the roll. A wonderful, protective friend, but not a lover.

She suspected he wanted it though. He'd never done or said anything even the slightest bit inappropriate, but on occasion, when he didn't think she was paying attention, he'd look at her with such tenderness and longing that it made her breath stop.

And her own body had started to respond to him. Just little tingles, tremors, rushes of warmth and unconscious, unprovoked thoughts leaving her a little aroused and breaking a sweat.

It all screamed betrayal and a twist of annoyance and depression brought prickles of tears to blur her vision. She shook it off and crossed the living room, Bokken ghosting her heels.

The moment she pulled the door open, she could see his mood. His aura pulsed around him in harried waves, the azure color shimmering and sparking in cool flames. The expression he wore told less, a practiced cop mask she alone could see right through. "What's going on, Alex? I didn't expect you today." A sudden thought had fear bolting up her spine. "Did everything go okay last night? No one was hurt?"

"It's fine. You were right though. There was a little girl." He nodded, frowning hard down at his worn boots before his vivid blue eyes caught and held hers. "I'm sorry for coming by without touching base first."

"It's okay," Relieved, Dana moved aside and he stepped past. He hadn't shaven, but the fragrance of his soap and some kind of spicy deodorant lingered in the air. "I have some work to do, but I have a few minutes."

He shifted toward her, opened his mouth before

closing it. Taking a step closer, he tilted his head, scrutinizing her. "You didn't sleep."

"I, um, well, not really." She shrugged. "Just one of *those* night." Turning away, she walked toward the kitchen, unwilling to let him see her face at that moment. The truth about what happened was close, but she didn't think it was worth letting out. He'd just worry. "Did you want some coffee? I just made some."

He followed her through the front room and into the kitchen, accepting the mug she poured out for him with a murmured thanks. Alex slid onto a bar stool and leaned on the counter. The muscles in his jaw pulsed in agitation and Dana inwardly braced for the impending storm as she eased onto the stool next to him. She expected she knew what was coming.

When he said nothing for too long, she cleared her throat and forced a smile. "Well, I presume you'll eventually tell me what brings you 20-odd miles and through my door before nine in the morning, right?"

His brows drew together and he frowned at her. Through her. "You're not the only one who didn't sleep."

Taking in the shadows under his eyes, her mouth quirked to the side. "I can see that."

"Thanks. Thanks, a lot." He responded dryly, staring into his coffee, but not drinking. "I feel like I'm stepping on eggshells here."

She frowned, but waited for the inevitable.

"I keep thinking about things," his baritone sounded rough, like tree bark.

"The answer is no. You've wasted your time." She breathed out a long rattling sigh that didn't even come close to relieving the tension. At his quick look and the darkening of his eyes, she hurried to smooth it over, knowing it would be fruitless, knowing she had to try. "I realize you're worried, Alex. I know you want me to stop. You think you're subtle, but believe me, you're not."

He blinked, surprise rippling over his face.

"It's obvious, at least it is to me." Dana dropped her gaze to her entwined, whitening fingers and worked to relax them. She hadn't meant to say that.

Alex gazed at her for a long few seconds before shaking his head.

"I understand you feel this … compulsion. I understand you want to help people. I get that. I really do, but it shouldn't happen at your constant expense." His voice lowered to a growl, a warning to anyone but her. "It's obvious you're getting weaker and weaker during and after every hunt. And I *know* you blacked out last night. And I *know*

you struck down Davey wanting to take you to the ER."

She pulled a deep breath in and let it out slowly, the flicker of a guilty smile playing around her lips. "He wasn't supposed to say anything because I know you worry too much."

"He might have a crush on you, Dana, but *I'm* still his boss." Alex took a swallow of his coffee. "Maybe you should just *consider* stepping back for a bit. Don't agree to every single one. Give yourself a break, a rest. Maybe even go in and get checked out. I could be wrong, but you're probably due for a doc visit anyway."

She'd already gone, enduring the usual tests. Her doctor had left a message she had yet to return. "I *can't* stop. You know that and you know why. I *have* to think what happened, happened for a reason. Losing Jesse, going through all that crap to scratch my way back." Dana shook her head. "Being forced to live with my dad for all that time, which was far from a picnic, I assure you. I love him dearly, but, well, I prefer my space. What

I can do is an amazing thing, Alex. Just thinking about that little girl last night, what could have happened to her if I'd decided to throw up my hands and said screw it, I'm done. 'You're on your own faceless, nameless child. Good luck.' Seriously Alex, what might have happened?"

"You said that some hunts are just harder than others. Maybe at one time that was true, but I don't think that's the case any longer."

Her attempt to make him understand bled away and when she met his eyes again, her stubborn streak burned up her backbone. "You don't know what you're talking about, Alex. There's no way you can know what this is like and what I have to contend with."

"No, I can't pretend to completely understand, but I can tell you what I see. In the beginning, you hardly broke a sweat and could bounce right back after a hunt. It was almost a high. Hell, for me, too. Now I see a woman barely conscious by the time she locates her subject."

"It doesn't matter. Besides, I'm fine now." She jutted out her chin, jaw clenching.

"It *does* matter. Damn everything, you need to stop hunting." His voice rose in temper and he slammed the mug on the counter. Coffee sloshed onto his hand and despite her own wince, he didn't seem to notice. He glared at her, his gaze intense, direct.

She narrowed her eyes and rose. Temper wasn't just prevalent for Alex. "It's not for you to say. I'm done talking about this. Now I have work to do. You should go."

Turning her back, her hip ached and she tried to hide it behind perfect posture. Fatigue, physical or even mental, always brought it on and Alex knew this. She didn't want him to feel guilty, at least not really, but it became evident in the tone of his voice.

"Dana—"

She started for the stairs, her dog shadowing her heels as always.

****

Alex couldn't leave this way. It would seep into his marrow and sting for days. He thought he'd be able to keep his cool. So much for that. Without taking a moment to reconsider, he followed to catch her by the arm and swing her toward him. The angry glint in her eyes shifted to confusion and something else when he cradled her face in both hands. "Please just think hard about this. You've done so much for everyone else and that's commendable. No one knows that better than I do. But your family needs you as well."

He stopped short of telling her he did, too.

"*I'm very aware of that.*" Her voice lowered, the edge softening. "Look, Alex. I know you made a promise, but Jesse is gone. I'm not your responsibility. Despite what you think, I *never* was."

Her words hurt, even though he knew she was technically right. But a promise was a promise and Alex couldn't pretend it didn't matter. "I care about you, Dana. I would even if…"

The thought hung between them.

Her skin felt so smooth and soft beneath his palms. Before he could stop himself, he ran one thumb across her cheek. Dropping his hands, he quickly stepped back, shame burning his blood. "I'm sorry. I guess I'd better let you get your work done."

Unable to meet her eyes, he pulled in a shaking breath before letting himself out. His anger had wafted away in a puff of steam. "Just think about it."

He pulled the door shut behind him, running a hand down his face. *Idiot.* He hadn't meant to press and, of course, what did he do?

With a small growl scratching his throat, he climbed into the cab of his truck, bringing the engine to life with the roar of diesel.

When he pulled away from the curb, his eyes flicked to the rear-view mirror, thinking, for just a moment, she may have opened the door to gaze after him.

Chapter Six

Charles Caras rested in his desk chair with one hand gently stroking the blonde locks of the child curled in his lap. The little girl had crawled up while he'd been on the phone a half hour prior and had promptly fallen asleep with her thumb poking in her mouth.

He'd forgotten to lock his office door and Olivia had slipped out from under her nanny's nose. Caras wasn't surprised. His daughter was a wily one. It made him proud at times. Now he was just annoyed.

Beyond the huge mahogany desk, Victor Alvarez sprawled in his chair, patiently waiting for the last several minutes. A perpetual twist of his lips led most to think he was in a constant state of amusement. They wouldn't be wrong, but it often hid other qualities. Dark, useful qualities, but ones Caras preferred to keep separate from his family.

"Sir, I'm so sorry." The young woman ran through the open office door, flushed, ginger hair pulled from her normally pristine twist. Her Irish lilt thickened in her distress. "I thought she was down for her nap and I was—"

Caras stared at her and her words puttered out. Excuses were not something he cared to hear. His staff knew that.

"Let me take her. I apologize again." She approached and held out her arms for the child, respect with a glint of fear bright in her eyes.

"It's fine, Penny." He stood, the child clinging to him, little fingers surprisingly strong in slumber. He took a moment to unhook them from his shirt. "But I can't have any more distractions this afternoon."

"I'll make sure of it." She took the girl, bundled her against her ample chest. A tiny protest slid out from between the three-year-old's lips, but it puffed out in a light snore.

Caras ran a hand down the child's back and followed the nanny to ensure the door was locked this time. He returned to his desk chair, leaned back and threaded his fingers over his stomach. He gazed at Victor who returned it without blinking. The man's tiny smile didn't ease.

"What do you have?"

Victor angled his head and let his fingers dangle to brush the handle of the briefcase beside him. "You want to see her? I've got photos."

"Not necessary."

"All right then." He threw his ankle over the opposite knee, relaxed. "29 years old. Car accident almost two years ago. Husband killed. Woman was comatose for nine days. Came out of it with a unique form of brain damage. Spent months recovering use of her right leg. After which, she started helping police locate 'Seattle's most wanted.' Supposedly, it's some kind of psychic ability brought on by the accident. From what I hear, no one's seen anything like it. Talk is she's all the rage in the medical journals." Victor grinned.

"Sounds outlandish." Caras tilted his eyes toward the open-beamed ceiling and sighed. It seemed ridiculous. He still remembered years back when vampires came to light in a manner of speaking. As far as he was concerned, that was just as ridiculous. Even more so. He'd had yet to see any evidence to indicate the media reports had been true. Next they'd try to convince the general public of Sasquatch and aliens. Gullible morons. This Chambers thing at least squeaked a little closer to plausibility. Facts did indicate she'd assisted in dozens of apprehensions and no one can be that lucky.

Victor shrugged. "My sources assure me she's the real deal. Fascinating woman. Quite beautiful, too, if you're curious."

"She might be fascinating to you, but she's dangerous. I can't have this woman pulling at the wrong strings. She's taken down three of my men."

Victor rolled his eyes and pulled a pack of cigarettes from the inner pocket of his jacket. Despite Caras's glower, he tapped one out and lit it. "Bottom feeders, Charles. They were stupid and careless."

"My nephew was one of them."

"I hate to be redundant, but Gabriel got what he deserved." Victor tilted his head with a tiny frown that was gone the next instant. He pulled on the cigarette and exhaled the smoke stream out his nose. "He didn't even work for you. He was just a freelance dumbass."

"I'm aware of that." Caras leaned forward, anger simmering deep in his marrow. "But he was *mine. They* were *mine.*"

Victor barked out a laugh. "So, if I get myself in trouble, you'll come riding to my rescue then? I'm sincerely touched."

Unsmiling, Caras stared. "And what happens if she starts sniffing her way up toward you, Victor? Your hands are far from clean."

"I find it unlikely, but as we're both very aware, you're the *boss*."

The word was a thinly veiled taunt and Caras pressed his lips together, irritation blooming. Victor held no fear of him. He was probably the only one who didn't. "Is there anything else? Any problems you foresee?"

Victor shifted, plucked something off his sock and let it fall to the Persian rug below. "Her security is excellent. Security glass, motion sensor lights front and back, solid door, intermittent patrol during the night, dog. She works from home. Not impossible to gain access, but definitely a challenge. Large margin for error."

"Suggestions?"

"I have some … people … who'd be willing to *help* if the opportunity arises." He smiled, teeth flashing white against his olive complexion. "The promise of big money can easily manipulate the simple minded."

"I gather these *people* are disposable?"

"Just more bottom feeders, Charles. Only with aspirations for something more. Amazing what some women might do for quick cash and the promise of a future with me." His grin didn't ease.

Caras regarded the other man with some distaste, but could see what a certain class of woman might see in him. Crow's feet spread out from dark eyes which always seemed to be laughing. He brushed his dark hair back from a high forehead, accentuating a widow's peak. A crooked nose, broken several times as a teen added some character, he supposed. Whatever it was, Victor was never without female companionship. "I'll leave it to you. Just make sure it's done."

"Sure, *boss*." He rose, stubbed his cigarette out against a crystal paperweight, grabbed his briefcase and strode toward the door. Pausing, Victor turned back. "So, when's the family going overseas? I'm surprised you wouldn't want to go with them until the matter is taken care of."

Caras shook his head, a long breath escaping him. "I can't spare the time."

"Yeah? I thought you just didn't like your in-laws."

"That, too." He allowed the barest smile.
****

Victor tossed his briefcase on the back seat and

climbed behind the wheel of his luxury sedan with its 700 horses waiting under the hood. His mind was already racing to the work and play ahead. The next few nights would involve sex, dramatic acting and subtle suggestions. He had several whores in mind and knew after the wining, dining, and mattress bouncing, most of them would be willing to do anything for him. *Anything.* Because, after all, they all thought they were his one special lady.

It was the best way to go, really. Women seldom suspected other women.

He chuckled as he threw the car into gear and left the Caras property with a little too much exuberance. The handling and power of the car made him hum in appreciation.

It was kind of a shame about Dana Chambers though. She really was a looker.

Chapter Seven

"Hi Dad." Dana pushed up on tiptoes to kiss her father's prickly cheek. "Forget to shave?"

Sam rubbed his jaw with one burly hand and grimaced. "Guess so. Better take care of that. Your sister-in-law will no doubt gripe about it after the fact. I can hear it now, *"Andy, your father didn't even care enough to clean himself up. He must be going senile!"*"

"She's not *that* bad." Dana clucked her tongue and stepped around him into the quiet of his front office. He closed it at 6:00 and Celia, his receptionist/assistant/right arm, had everything buffed to gleaming. Disinfectant had eradicated all traces of animal odor. Any cases which needed around the clock supervision had already been transferred to the emergency clinic and all borders held residence in the kennels and cattery adjacent to the main house. Jimmy, the kennel tech, would probably be out there now tending to them before leaving for the night.

Her father grumbled something to the contrary and Dana smiled. Rachel never said anything directly. She kept herself poised and proper at all times. Andy would be the one to say something later after his wife buzzed in his ear. Dana glanced at her watch. "Are they running late?"

"Yeah, yeah. You know how the boys are."

Her nephews were 5 and 7 and had turned procrastination and feet dragging into interpretive art.

Twice a month, the Cleary clan got together for dinner and conversation. It was one of the few things her father insisted on and, at one time, Dana enjoyed it. She loved her father and brother, adored her nephews and tolerated her sister-in-law, but since losing Jesse, everything felt strained. She always got the feeling Andy and Rachel stepped much too carefully and it made her want to scream. She only kept tradition out of respect for her father and fought the urge to cancel half the time.

She pushed through the side door and climbed the stairs up to the living area of the house with Bokken at her heel and her father not far behind. Her hip ached, but she did her best not to let it show.

"How are things?" Sam dropped into his recliner in his small, cozy living space as Dana settled into the corner of the couch. Bokken sat and rested his chin on her knee.

"Good, Dad."

"Headaches?"

She fought a sigh. "Not bad."

"Are you sure?"

Staring at him, she raised one brow and he softened, a smile curving his lips. "Sorry. Can't help it."

"I'm fine."

"Good to hear." He didn't believe her and Dana automatically clenched her jaw, releasing it, with effort, a moment later. "I worry about my baby girl."

"Yeah, everybody's worried about me. It must be a trend." She scratched her dog's ear, feeling cross and guilty because of it. She'd tried to keep her voice light, but without success.

Sam's old, fat beagle, Jasper, came wandering out of the front bedroom, sniffed a greeting to Bokken and plopped by the recliner. He let out a little howl for attention and Sam leaned over to run a hand over his head. "Everybody? Does that everybody include Alex?"

Dana said nothing, bristling inwardly.

"He wants you to stop hunting, doesn't he?"

"Yes. He came by this morning. Suffice to say,

we had words." She didn't mention the tenderness of his touch or the confusion burrowing into her gut.

"Does he have good reason?" Sam leaned forward, eyes sweeping her face. Concern sunk into the lines of his forehead, as always. "He's with you every moment when you … do what you do. What does he see?"

"He sees enough to overreact, but he doesn't understand." The pulse of a headache began a slow throb in her temple and she pressed her fingers to it absently. "I *have* to do this."

When he didn't respond, she glanced up at him. "I would think you'd understand at least."

"You can't save the world, honey." He reached out and touched her hand. "Have you considered that you've done more than your part? Maybe it's time to step away."

"It's not like I can turn it off." Having the same argument with her father was not something she'd planned on and as usual, she wished she'd cancelled out. She immediately felt like a creep. He was entitled to his worry.

"Okay, but in truth, how many people do you see actually merit police intervention? Are they the exception or the rule?"

"I…" She frowned and tried to gather her thoughts. Dark auras were uncommon, but she wouldn't exactly call them rare.

"You actively seek them out, right? It's not like you go to the drugstore and find yourself surrounded by criminals. Or do you?"

"No, of course not." she conceded, annoyed he was doing the same damned thing as Alex. "But last time I did help save a little girl."

Sighing, Sam twisted around and began filling his

pipe with tobacco. Soon, the scent of Dana's childhood would fill the room. "What you've done to this point is amazing. I mean, I wouldn't have believed it if you weren't my own flesh and blood."

"You didn't at first." At the time, she'd felt certain he'd considered having her committed.

"Well, you can't blame an old fart for being skeptical. Especially one with a scientific background." He struck a wooden match and lit his pipe, puffing the aroma of cherry. "But I admit my mistakes. You did prove me wrong."

Dana smiled. He didn't *always* admit his mistakes. He had too much pride for that. But he admitted them enough to provide balance to his two children. They knew he wasn't infallible. "But this isn't about me. The bottom line is, does Alex have a point? He hasn't said anything to me, but then again the guy would just as soon cut his tongue out than betray your confidence." Sam's relentless gaze cut into hers. There was something knowing in his eyes and she felt a trickling of warmth rise to her face. "What's been happening out there? What has him worried?"

"Dad—"

"And please don't bullshit me, Dana. You've never been good at lying, so don't try to perfect it now." He continued to stare and she shifted, uncomfortable.

The intensity of his expression had the years dropping away. She had to remind herself she was a grown woman and not the 7-year-old who'd dyed the cat purple. Her warnings from the neurologist tripped on her tongue, but she couldn't vocalize them. He'd lost her mother over twenty years prior and the thought of airing her worries burgeoned the emotional pain in her chest. She couldn't do that to him. "Look, I'll consider taking a break, okay? Maybe even take a mini vacation. Would that be acceptable?"

He narrowed his eyes and opened his mouth to respond, just as two little boys burst through the door to tackle him.

Sam wrapped an arm around both grandsons, but shot a pointed look indicating he wasn't ready to let it rest.

She figured she'd just have to scoot out before he had the chance to revisit. It just shoved back the inevitable, but she was okay with that.

Her youngest nephew slipped out from his grandfather's embrace and crawled into her lap, grinning broadly. He was missing two front teeth. "Hi, Aunt Dana!"

"Hi, Ben." She hugged him close and kissed the top of his head, careful to keep her emotions tightly clamped down.

****

"Hey, it's me. I'm sorry about the other day. I had no right trying to push you like that."

Alex spoke fast, his nervousness showing in his hurried words. Despite her smile, Dana kept her tone low and serious. It was a petty torment, but one she enjoyed. "I think you sometimes forget I'm not your subordinate."

"I know, I know. It's just that I—"

"Worry. I got that already." Dana pressed the phone between her shoulder and ear as she moved the mouse to direct the size of the graphic. The page came along nicely and she was positive her client would be pleased. "I appreciate it, but it gets on my nerves."

He let out a whoosh of air of his end. "Look, can we forget I said anything? I thought maybe I could swoop by and pick you up. We could go to that new place you wanted to try. We could just hang out, relax, and not think about this shit."

"What? *Tonight*?" Dana frowned, estimating her work load and the time she'd need to complete it.

"Sounds good. I'll pick you up at six." His clipped words smoothed out, a tiny bit of smugness creeping in.

"Wait. Did you just con me? I have work to do!" Somehow things had turned around and she didn't recall letting it happen. "I can't just drop everything."

"Of course not, but you have to eat."

"Alex—"

"I hear they have really good desserts."

"Now you're just being mean." She couldn't keep her smile out of her voice any longer. "But I have to admit, that's one hell of an offer."

"I'm sure your work can wait for one night."

"Tell that to Mrs. Taylor and her jewelry boutique."

"I'd be happy to. Give me her number."

"Okay, okay. Stop already." She guided the cursor to save her work as something slowly dawned on her. "Alex, is this, like, a date?"

His end fell quiet for so long she thought the call had dropped. When he finally spoke, his words were barely above a whisper. "Do you want it to be?"

Her heart tumbled into her stomach, excitement and guilt twisting together in uncomfortable pulses. Hadn't she wanted this? If she were going to be honest with herself, of course she had, but things had changed. Dr. Anders and his news had seen to it. It wouldn't be fair to Alex to start anything now. Anxiety soared and she closed her eyes.

Everything was so damned unfair. She wasn't perfect, but she wasn't a bad person. All this shit shouldn't have happened and it definitely shouldn't *keep* happening.

But how could Anders *really* know? The shadows on her MRI could just mean her gift was evolving. All her so called "experts" marveled practically from the moment she'd opened her eyes. After all, her condition and subsequent talent were unparalleled. Before she could stop herself, the answer slid from between her lips.

"That would be nice."

Chapter Eight

Shadow … shadow … boom!

The words repeated in her head, almost a military drill, or at least what she'd imagine one to be. It was just common sense. Watch carefully, don't hurry, be sure to wait for the perfect time. Otherwise, the risk of a fuck up multiplied.

That's what she'd learned from Victor, just in snatches of conversation when he'd allow his guard down. It was pretty rare when he did, so this past weekend she'd been touched to find he trusted her enough.

Tina Lewis stretched out in the driver's seat, trying to ignore the tingling of a butt losing its fight with the squashed and threadbare bucket seat of her ancient Toyota. She'd parked around the corner from the woman's house, just at the mouth of the cul-de-sac. She figured it would give her a good view to watch out for the small sport utility wagon or the cop's truck. With any luck, if she were careful and he was adequately distracted, she could follow without notice.

Victor had been so unlike himself and her heart had doubled over to tie itself in knots. Vulnerable was something she'd never associated with him before, but as she'd cradled his body with hers, he'd shared the one thing which gave him pause—a job involving women or children.

As awful as the woman was, he just couldn't bring himself to end her, despite what was expected of him. He'd nestled against her, his warm tears touching her flesh.

Tina could understand that and definitely respect

it. If she believed in such shit, Victor easily could have been born in a different time. He was too gallant, even chivalrous to exist in the 21st century. He was a hero, as far as she was concerned. Certain people did horrible things and it was his job to make them disappear before they could do even worse. But, killing a woman, even someone like Dana Chambers, wasn't something he could bring himself to do.

Oh, yeah, Victor had told her all about the woman. How she worked with old people, gaining their trust, before sucking them dry. What kind of person could do that? Seriously?

A wave of disgust pulsed through her.

It wasn't like Tina hadn't thought about killing before. Way back when, she'd started to take steps to see that her uncle never touched her again, but the fucker beat her to it. He'd been toasted the night of her 17th birthday and had taken a header down the steps. She regretted not causing it, but she *had* witnessed it. The snap at the bottom of the stairs had echoed in her head, the memory amplifying it. It had been a satisfying sound.

When she saw the black truck heading toward her, before making a left into the cul-de-sac, she ducked her head and pretended to fiddle with the radio. Mousy hair fell across her face, blocking it from view.

She glanced to her right, noting the vehicle pulling into the single driveway by Chambers's house. The blond guy climbed out and paused.

Tina sucked in a gulp of air, waited, then relaxed. He'd already headed toward the front door.

The idea of the cop pissed her off, too. How the hell could he not know? Shouldn't his instincts, radar, or whatever, clue him into this woman's game? Or maybe he was just thinking with his dick. Probably.

Her uncle had been a security guard. A guy with a

badge who thought he could do whatever the hell he wanted even if it meant trying to diddle his niece.

Chambers's home was the third house on the north side. A cute home that made the acid in Tina's belly snap with derision. So fucking unfair. She lived in an apartment in Burien and this bitch got to live over this way. How many old people had she swindled? Victor hadn't said, but his tone had been one of disdain.

One thing he had promised her, is that he'd help her get out of her crappy neighborhood. He'd cried even more then, apologizing that he hadn't thought to do it before. He had so many jobs to see to, so many shitty people to put down, it hadn't even crossed his mind.

She'd forgiven him of course. Victor was, indeed, one of the good guys.

****

"You cut your hair." Dana smiled a little Mona Lisa type smile up at him, eyes glimmering in tease.

Self-conscious, Alex raised his hand to his shorter locks. "Yeah, well, I guess it was overdue."

"You look good." She caught his arm and pulled him in past the threshold. "I like it."

"Thanks."

"Let me just feed Bokken and we can head out."

Both he and the dog followed her from the living room into the kitchen, watching as she measured out dog kibble and topped it off with a generous portion of wet food. Alex wrinkled his nose at the smell and Bo drooled on the floor.

Dana had dressed in a soft boat-necked maroon sweater, long suede skirt and medium heeled boots. Her make-up was light as always and her dark hair flowed untethered past her shoulders. It beckoned him to run his fingers through it, so he stuck his hands in his pockets. Tiny pewter feathers dangled from her ears and a matching pendant rested between her breasts.

As lovely as she looked, Alex frowned. "Is everything okay?"

She blinked, confused or just pretending. "Sure. Why?"

"You look a little pale." Her fair complexion seemed a little extra wan to him and when he met her eyes, he swore he saw discomfort flutter.

Lowering the pony-sized bowl to a grateful Bokken, she rested her hands on her hips and stared, as if weighing options. She then turned and fixed him with a brilliant smile that made his brain skip several thoughts. "I'm just a little tired, but looking forward to dinner tonight."

Recovering, he tilted his head. "Didn't you have an appointment with Anders recently?"

Dana's smile froze before turning small, sad, and making his heart ache. "Of course, Alex. I always have appointments with him. I am his pet freak, after all."

"Nowhere near." Alex shook his head.

"What would *you* call it?"

Her face crumpled before him. Shutting down his misgivings, he stepped forward to pull her against him. He cradled the back of her head with one hand and wrapped his other arm around her waist, securing her close, but not too close.

Relaxing into the embrace, she rested her cheek to his chest and Alex let his eyes dip. She felt so good in his arms, so right, so overdue. A current of disappointment fluttered through him when she began to pull away, stilling when she didn't go far.

Dana gazed up at him, dark eyes unreadable.

He didn't move, just stared back. Her light perfume teased his nose, the warmth of her body inches away. "Um, are you ready to head out?"

She nodded, a tiny crinkle appearing between her eyes. "We have a reservation?"

"We do."

Pausing, she seemed to come to some kind of inner decision. His breath stopped when Dana reached up with both hands to press against his cheeks, her gaze still on his. "You're a good man, Alexander Kelly, even if you are sometimes a pain in the ass."

He blinked in confusion seconds before she brought his face down to place her lips softly to the corner of his mouth, just a hint of a kiss. She stepped away to get her coat the next instant, offering him a tiny smile over her shoulder.

****

Dana fiddled with her straw, smiling across the small table. For the first time in too long, she felt relaxed, almost normal. Darkness and pain had retreated to some imperceptible corner of her mind and she was happy to leave it there.

Inside the restaurant, a relaxed mixed decor of modern and classic surrounded them. Bold primary colors of the walls and ceiling complimented elegant glossy black tables where oodles of patrons sipped drinks, ate, chatted, or drifted. A curved balcony horseshoed above the floor level crowd and dance floor, allowing more privacy with perfect views. Their own table pressed against the wall just to the right of the stage, which allowed Alex a view of both doors—the main entrance and one leading to patio dining. Of course, the place was so crowded, she doubted he could see much. He didn't seem to mind though, easy smiles slipping through his usual impassive façade.

He watched her, waiting.

Dana tilted her head, considering her childhood story, then reconsidering. She pushed ahead anyway.

"Okay. Years ago, my dad decided he wanted to bring his veterinary practice home. You know, so he could be there for my brother and me. While the house was being renovated, he kept the clinic in this little strip mall a few miles away. During the summer, I'd go along with him to work. I was, maybe seven at the time and, you know me, I always loved the animals, so I'd pitch in with what I could. Usually it wasn't much, maybe just wiping down some cages or tables, playing gofer for non-emergency, stuff like that." Dana stirred her daiquiri and took a sip, letting the sweetness overrun her tongue and rare alcohol haze warm her. She hadn't had to take any painkillers, so she figured she'd allow herself one. "One day I took some garbage to the dumpster out back and here I found this broken *horse-sized* dildo lying on the ground."

Alex started to grin and sipped his beer.

"I didn't have a clue what it was, so I brought it inside, not really noticing the gasps and laughter from the staff. I was looking for my dad, because he knew everything, of course. I find him out by the receptionist chatting with a client about her little Bichon." She giggled at the memory and took a breath to steady herself. "I tap him on the arm and wave this giant latex dong at him and ask what it was. I swear he turned purple. Even his *ears* turned purple."

Clearing his throat, Alex struggled with his own laughter. "Well, that must have led to an awkward conversation."

"No doubt. This old lady, Mrs. Krebbins – I think that was her name – oh, my God, I thought she was going to have a stroke right there between the dog cookies on the counter and the racks of prescription food behind her. Even the office cat, Mr. Tibbles, froze in shock."

Alex snorted and rested his forehead on his palm

for a moment, appeared to come to a decision. His brilliant eyes shone. "I've got one."

"All right."

"When I was twelve, my dad took me to the coast for some male bonding. Outdoorsy stuff, some hiking but mostly fishing. Anyway, I had this thing for buying random t-shirts and I found one that advertised a dive shop. It was so cool and I showed it to my dad and he just kind of smirked, nodded, and told me it was excellent and to go for it." Alex finished his beer, trying not to smile. "So, Monday morning comes around, I get up for school and decide to wear my cool new shirt. My mom takes one look, demands I change, and grounds me for two weeks. In fairness, my dad did intervene but, God, the look on her face."

"And what did this infamous t-shirt *actually* say?"

"Muffy's Dive Shop."

Dana coughed, the remaining drink spraying across her side of the table. Laughter rolled through her, eyes streaming and her incredulous question only squeaked out. "*What?!*"

"And she didn't believe me when I told her I honestly didn't know what it meant."

He chuckled across from her, his baritone wheezing as he tried to recover. Pulling in a few deep breaths, he caught her eye and they started laughing all over again. She had to admit it felt phenomenal, an easy exchange born from years of friendship.

****

A quintet of musicians on the center platform stage began to fill the night with smooth, smoky notes communicating a different time and place.

Alex pushed his chair out and rose. He held out his hand. "Feel like dancing?"

Jesse would just have to understand, wherever he might be. A teeny tiny part of Alex expected his old friend might even approve, but he couldn't tell if that part made excuses or was just awash in bullshit. He shoved the unpleasant thought aside.

"Dance?" Dana muttered the word as if it were a puzzle.

"Yeah, you know. See those people up there?" He waved a hand toward all the couples moving around the polished wooden floor. "They're dancing."

"If they were jumping off a bridge..."

"Depends on how high the bridge, how deep the water, and if I had a bungee attached."

She turned toward him, deep-brown eyes amused and annoyed. "Smart ass."

"What do you say? Take a turn with me? I promise not to step on your toes or if I do, I promise a free ice pack and foot massage."

She watched him as he continued to grin before lifting one shoulder and allowing it to drop. Dana allowed her own smile to match his. "Sure. I'll take the chance."

Chapter Nine

He led her through the buzz, crowd, and music, surprising her with a sudden dip that popped a laugh from between her lips. Pulling her up, he smiled down into her face and brought her into a close dance. A young vocalist brought a sultry edge to an Etta James standard and Dana felt the music swell inside and nurture that little spark she thought had died almost two years ago.

"They're really good."

Alex nodded, smile moving from his mouth to shine in his eyes just for her. He turned her, one hand around her waist, the other secure in hers. Dana gripped his shoulder, mindful of the lean muscles under her touch, perhaps too mindful, when the sound of her heartbeat and rasp of her breath filled her ears.

It had been so long. A slow progression from bottomless grief, to day-by-day, to noticing the sun again.

And he'd been by her side the whole time. She'd been comatose for the funeral, but Alex had driven her out to see Jesse's stone after her release from the hospital. He'd stood a discreet distance away as she said her formal goodbye, only ready to leave when she was.

Alex propelled her in slow circles, avoiding other couples with the ease of natural grace. He was just lucky she hadn't mashed a toe yet. Of course the evening was young.

He held her firm but gentle and a low tingle of electricity melded her to him at every point of contact. Brain fuzzing over, Dana stopped dancing and gazed up at him.

He halted when she did and now stared down at

her, while couples continued to move around them. Music meant to kindle emotion in the heart shrunk around the periphery as they stood enmeshed in a frozen hug from when their dance stopped.

His eyes flicked between hers, his face close enough to see the tiny scar above his eyebrow from a long ago bike accident, while the scent of his lingering aftershave tantalized her.

Dana held her breath, the action unconscious. She couldn't pull her gaze away.

Leaning down, he hesitated less than a moment before brushing her lips with his. It was more than her chaste, experimental kiss from before, but still tentative, careful.

She sighed, unable to retreat, unwilling to.

Alex kissed her again, barely a whisper, but the friction heated her mouth and spread across her cheeks.

He stopped to rest his forehead to hers. "Please don't cry."

She hadn't realized she was. Without acknowledging, she caressed his face, the prickle of his five o'clock shadow beneath the pads of her fingers.

Alex took her hand and moved them again to a new song, just as smoky and sultry as the last and pressed his mouth to hers once again. Just a tiny suck, nibble, melding and parting. She began to drown in him, in the slow dance, music and night. Everything became bright, surreal and she wondered if she'd take him into her bed tonight.

When the music shifted tempo, Alex touched her back and they returned to their table where their drinks waited. He seated her before taking his own, eyes still connected to one another.

"Is this why you want me to stop hunting?" She knew it was the wrong thing to say, but the question escaped before she could stop it.

He sighed. "I'd want you to stop regardless, Dana."

"I don't want to argue, especially now." She palmed her glass, the surface cold with condensation against her heated skin.

"Then we won't."

The waitress appeared with their meals, her smile a little too bright toward Alex as she openly perused him. Something dark and angry deep inside had Dana narrowing her eyes at the other woman.

"Can I get you anything else?"

He glanced at Dana who shook her head. "No, I think we're good. Thank you."

"No problem. Just so you know, your drinks and dinner are on the house tonight."

That made him lift his gaze from her to stare at the waitress, suspicion obvious. "Why would that be?"

"Joseph is here. He's the owner. Says it's on him." She jerked her chin across her right shoulder.

Alex following her motion, jaw sagging, rare shock sliding over his features. The silence stretched for several long moments, while Dana stared, puzzled. He finally sighed and shook his head. "I can't believe this."

The server hustled off and Alex pressed his lips together.

"What's the matter?" She looked over her shoulder, noting throngs of people milling in the vicinity, but one in particular caught her attention. He was classically handsome, bordering the line of too pretty, with etched cheekbones, an aquiline nose, deep-set eyes and blue-black hair clipped short around his ears and neck. His eyes landed on hers and he nodded before sitting at a booth in the corner behind them. "Do you know him?"

"Not exactly."

"I don't understand."

"Don't look too closely, Dana." Alex warned.

Curiosity kept her gaze on the stranger, studying him until she became aware of something lacking. Something no one else would notice except her. With a gasp, she whirled around to face Alex, heart echoing in her ears. "He's a vampire, isn't he?"

Blinking, he frowned, just a tiny crease between his brows. "They know how to blend. How could you tell what he is?"

"He doesn't have an aura." She'd never come in contact with a vampire, only knowing and hearing as much as anyone else in the general public. "How do you know him?"

A muscle flexed in Alex's jaw. "Kind of crossed paths a couple years ago."

She waited, but he didn't offer any more.

The feeling of being watched became pervasive and she chanced another glance to catch the man still locked on her. A tremor raced up her spine when he fused his eyes with hers. Their color shifted between gold, caramel, sky blue and translucent green, merging seamlessly from one to another. There was a whole world of history, present and future hidden in them and she wondered how old he might be. Or maybe she was wrong, maybe he was new and by default, not much older than she. Something seemed to fall inside her, her mind, her insides, but the cushioned vinyl seat remained beneath her, while one hand rested in her lap and the other pressed the edge of the lacquered wood of the table. A wave of drunkenness passed over her and she dimly remembered she hadn't even finished one drink.

"Dana!" A strong hand gripped her arm and she turned to blink at Alex, her brain muddled, thoughts scattered. His gentle fingers slid across her face and cupped her cheek. "Come on back. Try not to look at him."

She snapped to the present like an elastic band, embarrassment and anger vying for prominence. "What the hell was *that*?"

Alex dropped his hand from her face. "Best not to meet his eyes. Some of the stories happen to be true."

She stared at him. "Are you serious?"

"As an embolism."

Dana glanced back again, remembered, and turned away. "My father doesn't think they really exist. Thinks the media cooked up the whole thing for ratings or distraction."

"Sounds like something your father might say and it's a fair assessment. Unfortunately, it's wrong." Alex picked up his drink, swishing but not sipping. "I'm not sure of their numbers, but I know they're careful not to be spotted."

"You said it's safer for them? Why?"

"Think rednecks and lynch parties, but replace the lynching with sunlight induced spontaneous combustion."

"That's sick."

"Yeah, but not all that uncommon. Of course, I'm pretty sure the perpetrators get the worst end of it a lot of the time. We just don't generally find the bodies." He took a swallow and winced. "Maybe a subject change is in order."

"Maybe." It seemed so strange, like a glimpse into some dark graphic novel where the monsters truly did live. "Um, I'm going to run to the ladies' room, Alex. I'll be back in a second."

He stood when she did and Dana felt his gaze remain on her until she disappeared into the surrounding crowd to follow signs leading to a long hallway off the kitchen and toward the restrooms.

Her body shook and she wasn't sure if it was Alex or the brief but intense connection with the vampire. Either way, she needed to splash some cold water on her face and calm her breathing.

The ladies' room was packed and she had to excuse herself to find her way to the mirrors, wincing at the truth in her reflection. She looked a little tired, but pinpoints of color rose high in her cheeks and her lipstick had been thoroughly smeared to the edges of her mouth. Forget the vampire, Alex was responsible for the weakness in her joints.

"Oh, wow."

A woman beside her gave her a sidelong look and a smirk, perhaps reading between the lines. She applied some new powder foundation and didn't bother to glance her way again.

Dana wondered if Alex still wore her lipstick and if the color looked good on him. In the dim light, she hadn't noticed. Stifling a giggle, she cupped cool water from under the tap and pressed it to her face, repeating the movement as her brain lost some of its fog.

Drying off, she freshened her eye makeup and reapplied a light coat of lipstick when someone knocked into her from behind, banging her ribs painfully against the countertop.

"Sorry," the woman murmured and Dana stared up in the mirror, seeing too much make-up and stringy hair. She frowned when the woman's aura flamed from deep orange to red, to charcoal. She'd never witnessed that before.

What the hell?

Whirling around, she grabbed her clutch and tried to follow. All auras were specific to the person, much like a fingerprint and she never forgot one once she focused. Pushing through the door, she raked through the crowd, conscious of a cramp rippling through her lower back. Ignoring it, she caught a quick view of the woman spreading her darkness though the sea of benign color. She hurried toward the front entrance.

Stopping, it occurred to Dana she had no real reason to pursue. Besides, Alex was waiting. Remembering his words, she let out a little sigh. Sometimes it really was best to just let go.

Changing direction, she worked her way through the crowd when the cramp spread and shot wicked pain through her back and side. Gasping, she reached out to grab a railing separating the lower levels. Nausea erupted and she swallowed to keep her dinner down, while pebble-sized beads of sweat broke against her forehead.

Oh, my God. What *is* this?

Chapter Ten

Alex craned his neck in the direction Dana had disappeared before admonishing himself in disgust. Turning into a stalker was not something she'd appreciate.

But he couldn't help but gaze over that way once again, heart doing a little flip when he saw her leaning against the railing. The light happiness in his chest gave way to concern, then panic when he studied her face.

Pale. Painful. And she clutched the railing as if afraid to fall.

Someone's darkness must have pulled her in. God damn it! Despite her protests, it had to stop already.

Leaping to his feet, he jogged toward her, dodging around dozens of club patrons, fighting the urge to give one a shove. "Dana, are you okay?"

Dark eyes wide, she turned toward him, slow, unsteady and reached out a hand. "Something's wrong."

"Wrong?"

Her legs buckled and he caught her before she hit the floor, hoisting her slim body with ease and cradling her to his chest. A sharp cry of pain reached him and his insides contracted in response.

"This way. She can rest in my office." The vampire, Joseph, appeared at his elbow and led him toward the bar. Without thought, Alex followed. It was just like before when Davey had wanted to take her to the ER and she'd refused. She'd probably refuse again. Damned stubborn woman.

A short hallway led off the long bar and the man entered, passing the first door before pulling out keys to allow them through the second one marked "private" in black and gold block letters.

The office was spacious with floor to ceiling bookcases, and a flush marble fireplace directly opposite. A massive leather embossed desk in the center of the room took up a good chunk of square footage, while a black sofa stretched adjacent. Alex carried Dana directly toward the couch, gently lying her down before blinking down at himself in shock. Red smears coated his button-down and dotted his hands.

"Fuck! What the hell happened?"

She cracked her eyes open, licking her lips. "Not sure. Someone knocked into me in the bathroom. My lower back ... oh, my God..." She gasped and shuddered.

Rejecting decorum, he ran his hands over her, peeling up her maroon sweater, shocked at the clamminess of the knit. Her fair skin was coated in blood and the dark liquid continued to escape, onto her, onto the couch and spilling over. Trying not to jar her, he pressed the cushions down away from her flesh to see a small, deep puncture wound just under her ribcage.

"Call 911!" Alex stripped off his shirtsleeves and wadded it against the wound to try to stem the blood flow.

Joseph had backed away and when Alex shot him a look over his shoulder, the gravity of the situation was a grenade blast to the head. He was stuck in a room with a vampire and a woman in danger of bleeding to death. Trying to push down the panic, he kept his voice steady. "Please, Joseph. If saving your ass meant anything, call 911."

Dana started to slide away, trembling as shock took over. Alex brought one hand to her face. "Hey, none of that. Stay awake, okay?"

"Tired."

"I know, but keep those beautiful eyes open anyway. *Joseph*, what are you waiting for?"

The vampire had moved closer, his voice low, almost gentle. "She's dying."

"You can't fucking know that. Call an ambulance or I will make your life, death or whatever the fuck you want to call it miserable every single second you're in my city."

"It's not just the wound." Seemingly unbothered by Alex's threats, he kneeled next to the woman who stared at him, eyes crystal and terrified. "There's something else inside. I can smell it. Whatever makes her different is killing her."

Alex's shirt became saturated with her blood and it continued to pump out at each beat of her heart. With one hand, he fumbled in his pocket for his cell, dropping it to the thick carpet from the slickness of his fingers. He made a grab for it.

Dana's eyes slid shut, face paper-white against her dark hair.

"There's not a lot of time," the vampire whispered.

"Shut up." He hit the emergency number.

"I can save her. She won't be quite the same, but she'll be alive at least."

The call wouldn't connect and horror iced over him at Dana's short, rasping breaths. Blood continued to pool and overflow, the light blue of his shirt forever gone in a gush of her waning life. How much blood could someone lose before dying? Two liters? Or was that for a man? How much for a small woman? He couldn't think.

Oh, please, please, come on. He stared at the phone. They were in the middle of the city. *Why the fuck wouldn't there be a connection?*

"It's now or never. Do you want me to help her?"

"Bastard."

"She's almost gone. Whoever stabbed her was either experienced or lucky."

Alex gazed down at the woman, tears stinging his eyes. She looked back, dulling, but not gone and tried to smile. With little strength, she touched his face. "I'm sorry, Alex. You're my very best friend and I should have told you. Joseph is right. It was just a matter of time…"

She lost consciousness on the whisper of a breath. With a guttural cry, he threw himself backward. *Please, he couldn't lose her. Not now.* "Do it, just do it."

He scooted away until slamming into the nearest wall and tried not to look as the vampire leaned over Dana. Sinking his head into his hands, he balled his eyes up tight and tried to block out subtle and not so subtle sounds.

Gasping, following by a low, agony-filled moan. Thrashing with more energy than she should have had. Soft whispers. *His name.* Distinct in her voice, tainted with confusion and pain. Sucking. More gentle words from Joseph he couldn't make out and didn't want to. Alex pressed the heels of his hand hard into his eyes, concentrating on the throbbing and the sparkles of light the pressure set off.

A feral keening filled the room and it took him several seconds to realize the awful noise came from him. It merged the horror, anger and profound grief into something primitive and heartbreaking. This couldn't be happening. It just fucking couldn't. His throat seared and he cut the noise off before it drove him mad.

Hands now clamped around his head, his own agony filled his existence and he gave his hair several sharp tugs. His insides shriveled and he wanted to die alongside her. Maybe he should have just let her go. Now they'd both have to exist with his random and selfish decision.

Fuck, fuck, fuck!

The death rattle. A sound he'd heard once before and hoped to never hear again. This time it was coming from the person who should have been his future, if she would have had him, and he never pumped the balls to tell her the truth.

I did a great job taking care of her, huh, Jesse?

Joseph stood over him. Alex could sense it rather than hear it.

"I swear, you better not have her blood all over your mouth…" He barely recognized his own voice, somewhere between rage and anguish. He wanted to hurt someone, but even with his tenuous link to self-control, he knew a full-strength vampire could snap his neck before he'd be able to blink.

"I'll take care of her until she's awake and ready to deal with the changes."

"I can do that." Looking up, the naivety of his statement registered all over the vampire's face and he landed on a receiving look of pity. Some part of him was relieved to see no blood on the creature's face, although he wasn't sure how that made it better.

"She'll kill you."

Not acknowledging the words, he pulled himself back to the woman's side. Her lips were red with blood, slightly parted, skin eerily translucent with a fine network of blue veins pressing from beneath. She didn't look like she was asleep or unconscious, but she didn't have the waxy look of death either. Taking her hand, he pressed his cheek to her flesh, startled at the chill. "Jesus, I'm so sorry, so very sorry, Dana."

Eyes blurring, he pushed up and pressed a kiss to her cheek, remembering the softness of her return kisses from just, what? An hour ago? Less? How could everything go to shit in such a short span of time?

"Would you like me to have someone take you home?"

Joseph was being so proper, so helpful, so *human* and it made him sick to his stomach. "No."

"It will be at least 48, maybe 72, hours before she awakens and she will be ... *confused* ... at that time. I advise you stay away."

"Because she'll kill me." Hollow, he now felt hollow. What would the next second bring?

"She may not mean to, but then again, she might. It's hard to say."

"What was it like for you?" Now monotone. He asked the question, but didn't look up at the vampire, eyes still on Dana's still face.

"That was a long time ago."

"Somehow I doubt you'd forget something like that."

Joseph leaned against his desk, his arms folded to his chest, strange eyes unblinking. "None of us do. You should go now. You can't help her."

****

There had been rare occasions when a fledgling vampire awoke too early for the process to be complete. Usually they went mad and were dead within a few days. Of course, if that happened, the woman would take Alexander Kelly with her.

He'd been keeping subtle tabs on the man since *that* night, out of some vague interest, if nothing else. He still couldn't figure out why Kelly had saved him. It made no sense. Any other human would have left him to cook.

Joseph didn't move, debating.

He did owe the man. There were over two

centuries of human still inside to acknowledge that simple fact. But that wasn't the reason for his impulsive decision, at least not the primary one. It had been close to 70 years since he'd turned someone and it would, no doubt, be decades again. There had to be *something* that beckoned to him and he could sense that something the moment the woman had stepped into his line of sight. She was more than human, but he wasn't sure quite how, just that whatever *it* was, had indeed been killing her. He hadn't lied about that.

And she had known what he was with barely a pause. Unless they held a practiced eye, most humans couldn't identify vampires. At least not a well-fed one. His curiosity had been piqued and that in itself had startled him. It was something he hadn't felt in decades.

The timing of the entire situation proved quite interesting, though.

Stabbed in the ladies' room. Judging from the wound, Joseph suspected an ice pick or some kind of stiletto. Probably a hit. When Alex recovered his senses, he'd see it as well.

Whatever made her special, made her dangerous to someone.

And whoever that was, wouldn't be pleased at the recent turn of events.

Joseph almost smiled at the realization, stopping himself when Alex pushed to his feet, turning, eyes haunted.

"Two or three days."

"Give or take."

"Where will she—?" He glanced back, brows pulling down.

"She'll be safe. I give you my word."

"I'll be back." Alex stepped past, heading for the door. Joseph's firm hand caught his arm and held him before he could reach it.

The vampire kept his voice soft, trying compassion, hoping it fit. "You need to keep in mind, and I know you don't want to hear it, but everything has changed. For her, yes, but for you, too. She won't be the person you knew, at least not completely."

Alex stared down at the lush carpeting under his feet, said nothing before pulling away and shoving through the door into the hallway.

****

He needed a fight. Something to ease the burning rage and despair inside. Just a drunken insult or better yet, a good old-fashioned mugging. Something, *anything,* to release the steam of the pressure cooker inside.

As he sifted through the waning sidewalk crowds, it didn't happen. The walk back to his truck had been woefully uneventful. His fists continued to itch, needing to lash out and hit hard enough to smash a nose, or knock teeth out, or chip an eye socket, but there was nothing. Maybe he gave off unconscious but blaring warnings to whoever crossed his path "Do not fuck with me tonight. You *will* be hurt."

Unlocking his truck, he climbed into the lingering perfume in the cab. Light, floral, slightly exotic. It was all she wore and had for as long as he could remember.

"Oh, God. Please forgive me." The rage extinguished in a whoosh, leaving him weak and shaking. Tears stung his eyes and he pressed his palms against them. They'd been laughing together, dancing together, sharing first kisses, and now she'd been ripped from him.

Maybe it was just his punishment for being in love with his best friend's wife all these years.

Taking a few minutes to regain control, Alex threw the truck into gear. He had a freestanding punching bag in his garage and a pricey bottle of bourbon in his kitchen and fully intended to imbibe in both. But he had something else to do first because he knew Dana would want it.

Instead of heading home, he continued north, backtracking along the route they'd taken just a few short hours ago. He concentrated on his breathing and driving, the radio mute, the noise in his head unbearable, until he pulled up in front of her little house.

Without pause, he threw himself out of the truck and strode up the path leading to her tiny front patio. He let himself in with the key she'd given him months ago, quickly disarming the alarm and turning to the sound of nails on hardwood.

"Bokken."

The dog came close, but stopped, flattening his ears and whining.

Alex smelled like blood. It had oozed through his button-down to stain his t-shirt, slacks and skin. He'd hidden it under his coat, but the smell wafted at him, coppery, sickly sweet. "I'm sorry, boy. I know this is out of the norm, but your mom would want me to take care of you, at least until I can get you over to Samuel's—"

Sam. Fuck. What the hell was he going to tell her *father?*

Another wave of anguish sliced through him, aggravating the wound he expected would never heal. "Okay, let's get all your belongings, 'kay, Bo?"

The dog whined again, lowering his head and regarding the man from the corner of his eye.

Alex grabbed treats and the bag of food from the pantry, tossed feeding bowls in a reusable grocery sack and grabbed the leash from the peg by the door. "C'mon, buddy."

Bokken eyed him, tail down, but wiggling the tip.

"Let's go, Bokken."

Begrudgingly the dog obeyed, softly crying.

"Believe me, I know how you feel." Alex smoothed the big head and clipped the leash to his collar.

Chapter Eleven

Tina Lewis had the shakes. Nerves, fear, exhilaration and excitement all whirled in her belly, each vying for its turn.

She'd thought she'd fucked up. She really did. When the big, black truck had disappeared from her view, tears clouded her sight, despair turned her inside out. She could just imagine Victor's disappointment. Sure, he'd do his best to hide it, but it would be there, just around the edges.

But he'd called her, his voice relaxed, timbre playful as always. He said he knew someone, somehow that got wind of a restaurant reservation. It boggled her mind that he knew so many damned people, but then again, she supposed it kind of made sense in his line of work.

Not that her initial mistake mattered now. It was done.

Victor would be so proud of her. Hell, she was proud of herself. She never thought she'd be able to do it.

She could barely keep her car in one lane, she was shaking so bad.

Admittedly, she'd been a little wary about using the weapon suggested, but Victor said it was like cutting into soft butter. Subtle, fast, lethal. The woman had probably been dead within 15 minutes. Or maybe a half-hour. Either way, it wouldn't have been long.

Smiling, Tina replayed the events in her head. That bitch had never seen it coming. She'd been too busy making goo goo eyes and mushy face with that blond cop. When she'd gone to powder her nose or whatever, Tina had jumped at the chance. And, oops, now the bitch was history.

Like butter.

****

Victor sat splayed on the bench in the park.

Hours earlier, the playground before him would have been swarming with children, while parents and caregivers kept one eye on their charges and one eye on their cell phones. The day had been overcast but rainless, certainly one to take advantage of.

Gaze always moving, he spotted a single shoe stuck in the sand box and idly wondered if the kid limped home or if he never returned at all.

He had dim memories of this park from his own childhood. His mother, her face now blurry around the edges, had taken him here after they'd hurried from one of the surrounding homes. A man had shouted after them, his deep voice bleeding with acid. She'd been crying but had tried to hide it as she sent him off to play with the other kids. The playground had been different, more metal, less plastic, all sand instead of soft recycled rubber. He'd climbed to the top of the brick pyramid to use the slide on the other side, feeling powerful only to spot his mother's damp face. The power inside left in a sudden whoosh of helplessness.

Victor had hated feeling helpless. After his mother was gone, he'd taken steps to avoid the bottomless well. He'd also tracked down the man from that day. Blood was just a liquid like any other. It spilled just as easily, regardless of genetics.

Now, a late-night breeze sifted his hair back from his forehead, bringing the scent of burning Douglas fir with it. Lakeside homes would have their fireplaces ablaze to press back the cold. He pulled a deep breath in, enjoying the fragrance. He rarely lit his own, most of his time spent away.

He stared beyond the deserted playground toward the vastness of the lake. The moon made a token appearance to cast a cold reflection upon the surface only moments before the northwest clouds rushed back in to swallow the pale light.

She'd lost them, as he knew she would, but Victor was well connected throughout the city and suburbs. He had to be. A little extra nudge and she was back on track.

Well, in theory.

Tina had sent a text announcing, "Mission accomplished!!!" with numerous happy and dancing emojis accompanying it.

Victor didn't feel happy or like dancing, though.

He hadn't received a single report to verify the whore's claim.

When she now stepped up from behind him to wrap her arms around his chest, only through practiced discipline did he not pull away from her. Disgust brought a bitter taste to his mouth and mind.

"Hi, baby. Did you get my message?" Tina leaned over him, cloying perfume making it hard to breathe. The idea that he'd put his penis inside this wretch was repulsive, but Victor was always the professional. He'd never let it show.

"I did."

"Are you proud of me?" She leaned over to kiss him and he allowed it, even softening his lips to complete the con.

"Of course, darling." He rose, sure to reach to take her hand in his. "Walk with me?"

She smiled at him, her eyes almost level with his.

Trails spread away from the park, threading through dense, yet skeletal winter foliage, flanking the banks of the lake. Branches poked or waved at them as they distanced themselves from swing sets and slides.

Water lapped at the shore to their left as they strolled. The trail narrowed, forcing them to walk single file. Victor, always the gentlemen, allowed Tina to go before him, following closely as he reached into his inner coat pocket.

Like butter.

Chapter Twelve

Alex opened his eyes to varying degrees of darkness and a subtle shifting within.

Heart bursting into triple time, he pushed against the mattress and scrambled up toward the head board, hand flapping at the nightstand, searching for his gun or anything else he could use as a weapon.

"I'm sorry, Alex." Dana floated into the faint moonlight sifting through the blinds.

As his eyes adjusted and fear sharpened his senses, her silhouette solidified and she came into focus.

"Why are you sorry?" His vocal cords felt coarse, frayed. He willed himself to reign in his fear. He didn't want to be afraid of her, yet he was. But there was something just as strong, if not stronger, working at him. It was difficult to come to terms with his need to be near her and the primal instincts compelling him to put as much distance between them as possible.

Dana stepped closer and tilted her head, regarding him. "I didn't mean to frighten you."

Low and sultry, the tone of her voice snapped at his fear, driving it back as love and desire rushed in to replace it. "It's okay."

He must have blinked because the next moment, she crawled over him, hair tipping forward, brushing against his bare chest. His blood pressure spiked and she inhaled deeply, no doubt smelling his arousal.

Her lips hovered over his, but when they parted, the white of fang shown in the darkness.

Fear flared, but he wrestled it down. He leaned forward, sifted one hand into her hair and claimed her lips with his. His tongue caressed the coolness of hers and explored the ridges of her mouth with a gentle sweep.

She pressed down against him, passion replacing the tentative beginning and he wasn't surprised when he felt the sting of a nip. Their lips worked together in a flare of fever, tongues jousting, prodding.

Alex attempted to roll her onto her back, but she wouldn't allow it as she left his heated kiss and brushed her lips down his throat.

Thrusting down on him, she caught and secured his wrists.

Terror sparked while she kept him immobilized, licking the stubble coating his jaw and pressing her tongue to the throbbing of his pulse.

He bucked in an attempt to dislodge her, but the woman's once lithe presence was granite.

"Shhhh..." Her pupils bled into her corneas and he watched, transfixed, calming.

"Dana?" The word spiraled out from a tunnel as his mind pulled away.

"I'm so hungry, Alex."

She placed a delicate kiss to his lips before returning to the evidence of his frenetic heartbeat.

The pain was sharp, but diluted quickly.

Dana released his hands and he traced them over the curve of her spine and then back into her hair, twisting his fingers in the satin locks, before they weakened and dropped to his sides.

Eyes dimming, he would have floated away if it weren't for the solidity of her body holding him down.

The night beckoned and her whisper followed him into its vastness. "I'm sorry, Alex..."

Alex awoke with a start and it took him several seconds to realize he was alone. Normal sounds settled around him, the low motor of the refrigerator, the click and hum as forced heat pumped through his home. The musical introduction to the quarter hour from his grandfather clock reached his ears and pushed through his rapid breathing.

"God!" Sweat ran from his pores, soaking his bedding, as his muscles shook in tension and horror. One hell of a nightmare. Maybe the seduction hadn't been real, but the vampire she was on her way to becoming certainly would be.

Nothing he could do would ever change recent events into a figment of his imagination.

Last night Dana had been stabbed and Alex had given a vampire permission to change her.

She hadn't had any say in the matter. It had been a rash and selfish decision that would have repercussions he couldn't even be able to foresee at this point.

He couldn't even imagine what he'd been thinking. He should have just tried to call 911 from the landline.

And with the rush of blood pooling around her, she would have been dead before the EMTs could arrive.

You don't know that.

"I was terrified to take the chance." He said the words aloud to the emptiness of the house.

It was too late. He could try to figure out *why* it happened to begin with or more appropriately, *who* was responsible.

A hit. Pure and simple.

But what the hell did it even matter?

Alex threw his legs over the side of his bed, hung onto the edge with fisted hands and stared straight ahead. The sun poked between the blinds, its brightness unusual against the more prevalent grey of the northwest.

His mind wandered to the present. Was Dana awake yet? No. Of course not. What had Joseph said?

Two or three days? How would she react? Would she remember anything?

It was possible she might emulate her maker by blending in and returning to semi-normalcy, but then again, how did that even work? Had Joseph been able to blend right away? How old did a vampire have to be to perfect it? He had no fucking clue. Alex could count the vampires he'd met on one hand and still have fingers folded. It had just been plain dumb luck or, perhaps, grave fortune, that had introduced him to Joseph the night of Jesse and Dana's accident.

Too many damned questions.

He needed to run. He had to pump all this adrenaline and frustration from his body. Part of him regretting dropping Bokken off with Dana's father. The dog would have been a good exercise partner, but it was for the best.

His visit had been brief and he'd fabricated a lame story about Dana being knee deep in work and needing Sam to look after the dog for a few days. The man hadn't believed him, it had been very evident in those deep green, piercing eyes, but like a chicken shit, Alex had taken off before he could be interrogated.

Shame and anger collided and he crossed to the dresser to pull on his sweatpants.

****

Joseph folded himself into the armchair across from the single bed, gaze affixed to the young woman in his care. The vivid crisscross of veins pressed from beneath her skin had slowly disappeared as her system reorganized and rebuilt.

Unable to stand the aroma of all that blood, he'd cleaned her up the best he could and swapped out her ruined skirt and sweater for a clean pair of jeans and a sweatshirt he'd borrowed from an employee locker. They were a little too big on her, swaddling her into the appearance of a young child, but at least he didn't have to suffer through all that savory temptation. Licking the blood from her skin would have been humiliating.

He'd kept her in the windowless room adjoining his office in the club, secure in the reinforced space accessed from behind his wall of bookshelves. It was a place he'd spent many sunlit hours when he hadn't wanted to make the trek to his primary residence. The last couple of days had been no different. Unwilling to leave her alone, he'd slept on the plush carpet beside the bed.

Not for the first time, agitation skittering under his skin in a nonstop circle since *that* night.

The moment he'd lifted her into his arms, he could feel the low vibration of power emanating from the girl's very presence. In all his years he'd never felt anything like it and the knowledge unsettled him.

More than once he'd contemplated leaving her outside for the sun to dispose of, but couldn't bring himself to do it. Her soft, beautiful features beckoned to him and the power inside honed her allure. He could barely pull his eyes away, let alone murder her.

What was it? What human gift did she bring with her?

It wouldn't be much longer before he found out.

He leaned closer to the girl, resting his forearms on his thighs. "What *are* you?"

The barest moan escaped her lips and her eyes moved behind her lids as if in the midst of an intense nightmare. Joseph stiffened, watching her closely, worry tickling his insides.

She quieted and after several long moments, he relaxed.

Not quite yet, but it wouldn't be much longer.

****

Dana couldn't quite reach the surface.

She'd been immersed in darkness far too long and had lost all sense of direction.

Panic and desperation squeezed the breath from her, but there was something else. An unfamiliar longing and hunger sat on her periphery like vultures waiting for death. Flickers of outside sounds reached her ears. The soft slide of footsteps, low thumps of a closing door, and the occasional whisper of a voice she didn't recognize.

Images rolled behind her eyes, some quick flashes, some longer and more painful. A man's face while driving, tense, upset. Bright headlights. A scream. Had it been her? Other snapshots. An older man with thick silver hair. Children at a backyard barbeque by a lake. Hers? No. Not hers. Nephews. A middle-aged woman with dark eyes and a kind smile, lines in her face deepening. Death mask. Tombstone. Mother. Another man with dark blond hair and brilliant blue eyes. Tenderness. Intense pain.

Scents invaded her nose. Paint, carpet, varnish, cologne, alcohol, food, and blood. Faint but there. The hunger rumbled.

Someone was speaking. The unknown whisper from before. A man's voice. Gentle. Well spoken. An accent so faint, unrecognizable.

A rumbling deep in her chest had her eyes flying open. The darkness disappeared and she broke surface with a gasp bordering on a scream.

Shifting, hazel eyes in an elegant face gazed down at her and she shrank away, the rumbling inside graduating to a deep growl.

"I know you're confused."

She stared, scrambling for distance and pressing her back into the wall behind her. Fight or flight rose within, but there wasn't any kind of debate. She had to get away. Her body shook, a need like no other wrenching her insides, threatening to pulverize her organs if she didn't … what? Didn't *what*? Panic lanced through her. Was she hungry? Horny? Yes and no. It was something much more ancient and primal. How was that even possible?

Eyes darting, she debated the odds of getting past this man to the door behind him. The night would spread out and she could disappear into it.

"You're not alone, Dana. I know what you're feeling." He reached a hand out and she had the urge to rip it off the end of his arm. There would be blood. Lots of it. The thought repulsed yet excited.

She leapt off the bed in one smooth motion, reaching out for the door handle just as iron bars wrapped around her body. No, not metal. The man had her, holding secure, almost painful. He was so strong and she couldn't pull away. Panic electrified her.

He'd backed her into a corner, forcing her to fight when she only wanted to flee. Growling, she snapped at him like a rabid dog. "Let go!"

"No. I am your maker. You must feed from me first."

Nothing made sense. This man was obviously insane. She struggled harder, but couldn't break free. His hand cupped the back of her head, forcing her closer and into the crook of his neck.

She tried to get her hands between them, wanting to shove him away. The smell of his cologne burned her sinuses, making her gag. Too much. Too strong.

Underneath it another scent caught her attention. One of meat, blood, and bone. Her insides rumbled and her salivary glands overflowed in anticipation. Her body knew something her mind wouldn't accept.

"Feed." The man's voice remained gentle, but the order was clear.

"Please let me go," she whimpered.

"I can't. Do as I ask."

Instincts rose along with the hunger. Her fortitude weakened and she let go, the smell of his flesh and blood overwhelming and undeniable. Dana bit hard, deep, his blood running pungent and sweet. What was hesitant became greedy. His power flowed into her, her mind floating, joyful, every foul memory dispatched in the moment. She pressed in closer, trying to rip the flesh even more, her wickedly sharp canines sinking in without hindrance. Looping her arms around his back, she clung to him, wanting, needing more, the animal unleashed and unwilling to be caged.

"Enough." He pushed her away.

"No, it's not." Dana pressed close, but he held her at arm's length, eyes wary, alight with … was that fear? She barely registered the strange reaction, intent on burrowing her way back against his throat.

"I said, enough!" A deep vicious growl of warning vibrated through him. Dana stopped, hair standing up on her body and coldness washing through her. The need was satiated, the painful rumble within gone. Confusion and fatigue settled around her and she stumbled back, trembling and unable to look at him.

He stepped forward, strong hands on her again, holding her biceps, before skimming around her back. "I'm sorry, Dana."

"Sorry…" *Think, think.* Where was she? Something had happened and the jumble of thoughts colliding in her brain wouldn't stay still long enough to allow her to piece it together. "I need…"

"What do you need?"

She hadn't meant to say it. Whatever it was, it

was premature. All she knew is she needed to get out of this small room. It was too hot, too stifling. The night waited. Home waited. Alex waited.

Alex?

The man stood before her waiting, arms around her. It was much too intimate. She couldn't remember his name.

And she'd just bitten and fed from him.

A moan seeped from between her lips and the prospect of escape wrapped itself around her once more. "I need to leave. I need to get out of here."

"It'll be dangerous."

"I'll be all right." Her voice sounded thin and unsure to her own ears.

He gazed down at her, his expression appeared to sadden. "I meant for everyone else."

Oh, God. Oh, my God. What *was* she? Shaking her head, she tried to push away. When he didn't release her, a deep belly growl erupted and she lashed out, hard enough to send him flying backward, denting and crumbling the dry wall to reveal the glint of metal.

She jerked open the door, blinking at the other barrier before shoving it aside and stumbling into an outside office. A long leather sofa took up one wall and she stared at it. In someone's arms. Pain. Cold. Tears. Darkness.

Backing away, she reached for the outside door and spilled into a hallway, following it into the suffocation of a crowd, the smell and sounds painful to her senses. Several people stared when she darted through, looking for the exit. A neon sign and smoky glass beckoned and she was within a few yards when the man appeared beside her again.

"Leave me be!" She snarled and a few more passersby turned toward her.

A manacle clamped on her wrist and he leaned in, voice gentle in contradiction. "The rules have changed now, Dana. Sunrise will drop you and you will die. You need to make certain you have shelter."

"I'm going home." She glared up, hating him, but unsure if he deserved it. Without waiting for a response, she yanked free and slipped outside.

Chapter Thirteen

Mario Rivelli was fed up. Instead of curling up with Judy Bosom (actually Beston, but he liked to twist it into her best feature) against the rawness of mid-winter, he was staking out some bitch's house in Green Lake. Three fucking nights he'd sat waiting to catch a glimpse of Victor's prize, but there was no sign of her. The only thing he had to show for his time was a cold and a possible hemorrhoid.

He tipped back a bottle of cough syrup and followed it with a swig of coffee. The idea was to feel better but remain alert. With any luck, they'd cancel out one another's negative effects.

Slumping down, he reached over to tinker with the radio, hoping to find one good song in a sea of crap. Nothing. Instead, he leaned down to paw through the CDs in the center consul. Making a choice, he popped it in the stereo, swaying his chin to the music filling the old car.

When he caught movement from the corner of his eye, he almost dismissed it, but fear of Victor's wrath had him reconsidering.

A kid turned onto the path leading up to the little house, stopping to stare up at it.

He thought it was a homeless kid at first, dressed in baggy jeans and a sweatshirt, but when she shifted and he caught a glimpse of her profile, he sucked in a breath and scrambled for the photo on the seat to compare. Pretty, slender with dark hair.

Yup. That was her.

She approached the front door and climbed the porch steps with such grace she seemed to float.

At once unnerved and intrigued, Mario grabbed for his binoculars to study the woman with a closer eye. Her hair was mussed, but her skin looked milky smooth and her eyes roamed back and forth, as if searching. She stopped and seemed to fix right on him. Something about her expression dried out his mouth and added a few extra beats to his heartrate.

There was no way she could see him. He'd parked in the shadows and the car he drove was as generic as they came. There wasn't anything to grab attention.

Still, she continued to stare in his direction.

Unconsciously, Mario held his breath, aggravated at the fear leeching into him. Seriously, what the hell? He wasn't a small guy by any means. Frequent gym visits brought up his bulk to about 236 on a six-foot-four-inch frame. This woman … this *little girl* … shouldn't have caused a single blip on his radar.

Then why the hell was the hair on his arms standing straight up?

To his relief, she dropped her gaze and turned to let herself into the house.

Pulling his cell from his pocket, Mario called his boss.

****

Dana soaked in the front room, familiar but somehow distant. This was her house.

It just didn't feel like it.

A variety of aromas floating on the air, cleaning solvents, potpourri, fruit ripening on the counter, faint perfume, dog.

Her eyes swept the living space, ears picking up nothing indicative of another living creature. Vaguely, like the earliest thump of a headache, she wondered where the dog was.

Stopping, her attention focused on every photo the room showcased. There were dozens decorating the walls, end tables and spreading their memories across the mantle. Smiling happy photos. Studying them, sparks of familiarity popped within her brain. Several wedding shots around Lake Washington. Her husband sitting on the back deck of the house with a beer and his guitar, her father, brother and sister-in-law on her dad's boat, nephews smiling gap-toothed smiles from their school pictures, the dog as a puppy. Bokken, that's right. All these snippets of life and time shot adrenaline into her fuzzy memory.

Another photo caught her eye. Jesse and Alex at some kind of backyard barbeque.

She stepped closer and reached out a trembling finger toward the image, pulling away before she made contact with the glass.

Jesse was dead. Gone forever. She focused on Alex, tunneling in on his face.

It was a good face. Handsome, a little weathered.

What had he done?

She remembered gentle kisses, blinding pain, being scooped up into strong arms, his terrified eyes … and then there was a stranger.

The stranger she'd fed from earlier.

He's a vampire, isn't he?

Dana let her eyes droop shut and pressed the heels of her hands against them.

Truth she'd attempted to push away settled down around her, dark and suffocating. Despite everything, she didn't want to entertain it, hoping against hope that this was some kind of intense nightmare and she'd wake up to the sun warming her face.

Instead she'd awakened to fear, confusion and a hunger like she'd never experienced before.

I am your maker. You must feed from me first.

A guttural scream ripped from her throat and she struck out to sweep all the photos off the mantle in a succession of crashes. Unsatisfied, she whirled and took her aggression out against her furniture, splitting wood with a single blow, tearing fabric, and shattering glass. Grasping one fireplace tool after another, she imbedded them in the wall with little effort. She flipped several bookcases, their contents sprawling across the floor to snarl with the sea of shards. She stepped through the mess, not losing traction as she whipped from one end of the room to the other, entering the dining room, kitchen and leaving physical and emotional destruction behind her.

Something inside needed to get out and since she couldn't identify what it was, she kept moving and wrecking, despair and fury whistling in her head.

Some dark, cynical part of her reminded there was an upstairs, too, but she stopped, dropping into the mess and trying to weep.

Nothing.

She thought about the persistent darkness outside. The aura she'd sensed the moment she'd reached the house. Someone awful was attached to it, but there was no telling if it had anything to do with her. She couldn't just go around sucking dry any criminal as she saw fit. The moment the thought surfaced, she realized she was, in fact, hungry again. That primitive pain and rumble inside shot clear to her skin.

Laughter bubbled up and spread over and through her. She suspected most of it was hysterical, but it didn't really matter. She'd gone from one extreme to another, surprised the abrupt shift didn't give her whiplash.

The thought just made her giggle harder.

Laughter or insanity. Or maybe both.

The shimmer of broken glass caught her eye and she crept through the devastation of her home, unmindful of the pricks of pain in her palms and knees. Photos of her life sprawled before her in various states of ruination. The urge to weep rose again and she cursed her short temper. She brushed glass from the smiling faces of Jesse and Alex.

Gone and forever out her reach. Both of them now.

But did that have to be?

Her stomach jerked in spasm and she curled forward. The hunger became more persistent.

How could she reach out when she might just eat him?

Laughter surfaced again.

Without looking up, she blurted out the question between giggles. "Are you following me?"

Dana had neglected to fully close the door and she could sense her maker on the other side. He pushed it in with one finger but didn't enter.

"Like it or not, you're my responsibility."

"Wonderful. Thank you for that." She glared at him, the sharpness of anger tainting her common sense. "Now what? Are you going to show me the ropes? Turn into some kind of monster mentor? Isn't that what I am now?"

He kept his expression blank, not outwardly responding to the bait. "You haven't fed enough."

"Sorry. Didn't notice any 'McBlood's' or 'Blood King's' on the way home."

Joseph frowned, dark brows pulling down, eyes glinting. A moment later, it all washed away. "Please don't starve yourself. You don't want to go down that route."

Her gaze fell back to the photo, even as pain

bolted through her insides. "Dead things don't need to eat."

"Dana."

Something in his voice had her glancing his way. Still not entering her home, he held out his hand, face softening. "Please."

"Why are you just standing there like that?" As soon as the question left her lips, she understood.

Some of the stories happen to be true...

"You can come in." It made no difference any longer. What more could he do to her?

He slid through the entry and crouched next to her, gaze searching and holding hers. "Dead things rot away. We don't."

"Okay, so I'm some kind of reanimated super corpse because I'm fairly certain my heart's not beating."

Sighing, he took her hand and pressed it to his chest. She tried to pull away, but the elegant fingers trapped her, too strong for her to escape. "It *is* beating."

She sat in silence, trying to feel it. When she did, it was like finding a single dot of Braille for the newly blind—she almost didn't recognize it for what it was. His pulse was down to perhaps five beats per minute, but it was there. Surprise rippled through her.

"We absorb our energy from feeding and everything around us. Our hearts barely need to beat."

"Is that some kind of load of crap *your* maker handed you?"

Joseph's movement blurred and his fingers curled around her throat. The discomfort bordering on pain was real. "Watch yourself, Dana. Don't make me sorry I saved you."

At that moment she had no doubt he could physically remove her head from her body. She clutched his wrist with both hands, defiant stare meeting his and holding. "Why *did* you? I'm nothing to you."

He peered at her for what seemed a very long time. Not responding, he finally released her. "You need to feed. You can't pass for human if you don't."

Frowning, she took a moment to register what he said before shock chilled her. It hadn't occurred to her to take a peek at her reflection since vanity wasn't currently a high priority. "I ... don't look ... like me?"

Joseph picked through the mess on the floor and found a broken piece of mirror. Face grave, he held the shard out to her.

With a shaking hand, she positioned it before her, the woman looking back distorted in the spider webbing. Dark smudges coated her too pale face around her cheekbones and eye sockets, but the black overflowing from her pupils and coating the entire cornea horrified her and she threw the glass aside. "Oh, my God."

Joseph grunted. "Meticulous make-up, sunglasses and intense *discomfort* ... or just feed."

Her stomach clenched again, this time hard enough to push out a gasp. "I don't know if I can."

Climbing to his feet, he studied her, expression what? Compassionate? Pitying? She couldn't tell.

****

The woman looked up at him and despite the ravages of hunger, a very human misery stared out from within. He did empathize, but at least his blood had given her some control. Furniture destruction was something she could live with—the deaths of loved ones wasn't. His own turning had included little guidance and he'd returned to his childhood home with very poor results.

When he'd arrived, he could feel that disconcerting buzz of power emanating from her and even as he stood there, it vibrated into his body. The part of him regretting his decision to change her had shifted into intense curiosity. Now, gazing down at her, he knew he wouldn't leave the girl. He needed to see how it ended. If he lost his existence as a result, well, he was okay with that. 267 years of life could be considered more than ample.

"Come with me. We both need to feed." He reached out to her.

Dana didn't take his hand, giving him a narrow look.

He could feel his own need growing inside, distant but shaping. Soon his appearance would morph into a visage capable of terrifying. Trying not to allow his impatience to show, he waited.

Rolling to her feet, she managed a little nod and followed him from her home.

****

Mario didn't complete the call, phone dangling from his fingertips as he watched the scene through binoculars.

The woman was loco. At least that was his first impression while he watched her destroy her living room. Parted blinds allowed glimpses of furniture being tipped, lamps thrown, glass shattered. He watched fireplace tools thrown with such ferocity, they stuck in the damned wall. And this wasn't one of those new tissue paper built houses either. It was solid from the 20s. What she managed to do would take tremendous strength.

Fear tickled the back of his neck, but he continued to watch, hoping to hell she wouldn't come out and pay him a visit, embarrassed in the realization.

When the dark-haired guy arrived, Mario sunk as low in his seat as his bulk would allow.

He had always been a man who survived by his instincts and right now they were telling him to get the fuck outta there. But he couldn't. Not yet.

Deciding to complete the call, he waited, tapping his thick fingers against the bottom of the steering column. *Come on ... come on...*

"Yes."

"It's me. Got some weirdness at the woman's place." Mario shifted, but kept his gaze fixed to the house, fearful he might get a nasty surprise otherwise.

"Weirdness?"

He recounted what he'd observed and Victor grunted. "Her visitor arrived by car, I take it?"

"Yup. Expensive one, too. What do you want me to do? Should I take them out?" Even as he asked, he hoped for an emphatic 'no' from his boss. Something was not kosher in the air tonight and Mario really wanted to see Judy Bosom again.

"No. Just stay put. If they leave, tail them. This little girl has me intrigued now."

"You got it." Mario responded, keeping the sourness out of his voice. So much for a pillow of big tits in the near future. He almost disconnected, but his heart popped in his chest before making a run. "Holy fuck!"

"Problem?" Victor remained calm as always.

"You're not gonna believe this!" He gasped, wondering if he very well might have a heart attack. "She looks different!"

"Different?"

"Man, she looks like some kind of fucking ghoul or something!"

His boss went quiet, the stretch elevating Mario's panic. He concentrated on breathing.

"Just follow them and let me know where they end up. And Mario?"

"Yeah?" He was dismayed to find his voice had elevated to that of a frightened woman and he fought to bring it back down.

"Calm down and don't get yourself killed."

"Uh, yes, sir."

****

Victor hung up on the hysterical man and stared into his drink. From the corner of his eye he could see the fire he'd chosen to treat himself to earlier had now reduced to a few burning embers. He considered throwing another log on, but the thought lost itself in the new batch flooding his brain.

Interesting.

If Mario wasn't hopped up on something and seeing things, the situation may have just made a dramatic new turn. Maybe Tina really had done the deed after all. It just happened to be at the wrong place and wrong time or perhaps, the right place and right time depending on one's point of view. Not that it mattered for her. She'd been one of many fated to be disposable.

Quentin, the big Maine Coon, strutted into the front room, surveyed his kingdom before leaping onto Victor's lap. He stroked the soft fur thoughtfully, while the cat kneaded his linen-clad leg and purred.

Considering the shroud of secrecy they lived by, Victor didn't have a lot of experience with vampires. A rogue had called attention to the species a couple decades back and although he suspected that that particular vampire had been either eliminated by its own kind or by a group of vigilante humans, the damage had been done.

The new development might prove a bit more problematic, but also much more exciting and profitable.

Victor sipped his drink, savoring the smooth flavor and the heat spreading through his veins. The cat curled between him and the leather arm of the chair and captured his hand to keep him secure in his petting duties.

Chuckling, Victor envisioned his employer's face. Aggravation of an incomplete job, but probably not fear. That wouldn't occur to him.

Well, he didn't know a lot about killing vampires, but he could fix that. He knew of someone who held a thriving livelihood of pest extermination. He just needed to talk to Caras first to revise his payment.

Smiling, he removed his hand from his cat's clutches and poured himself another drink.

Chapter Fourteen

Joseph steered southwest, guiding his late model luxury sedan down 99, passing over the Freemont Troll and cruising across the George Washington Memorial Bridge to arrive in the elite Queen Anne district.

Dana scarcely paid attention, the pain in her body twisting and turning through her muscles, punishing her stubbornness and sapping the strength from her body. Her mind, on the other hand, sprinted and stalled in a continuous loop. She'd wanted to find Alex, his aura reaching out and beckoning, but fear and instinct brought her home instead. Remembering Joseph's warning, she expected it was safer for her to stay away, at least right now. The demolishment of her furniture proved his point.

She wasn't even sure how she got home. It had been a rush of wind slapping her face and pushing her hair back. It would have been exhilarating if she'd felt free to analyze it, but everything was too much. Too bright, too loud, too angry, too horrifying, too overwhelming and a zillion other things that were barely a whisper against her brain.

Resting back against the headrest, she tried to shut her thoughts down but they roamed free, taunting, somehow aggravating the hunger burning within her. Shame sliced through her at the realization. Just like any animal, survival was priority and her body made sure she knew it.

Joseph pulled up to a walled property and tapped a code onto the available number pad. After a brief moment, the wrought iron gate swung open on well-oiled hinges to allow them entrance.

An impressive Tuscan style mansion spread out

before them. Elongated arched windows gave the home a surprised appearance while the gently sloping roof topped with Mediterranean tiles contrasted with brilliant white stucco.

Guiding the car up the driveway, Joseph cast several glances her way. "When you feed from your maker, he shares his physical and mental strength, but, unfortunately, you do not receive essential nutrients you need."

"So … you were just sort of an energy drink," she murmured.

He laughed, the sound unexpected, even pleasant. "That certainly is one way to look at it."

Not reacting, she fixed her gaze straight ahead. "Where are we?"

"A friend's."

"Some kind of blood bar?" It sounded ridiculous, but she didn't know how it all worked. She'd expected to prowl the back alleys of downtown for an unsuspecting victim.

Joseph chuckled again. "Not quite."

She started to say something else, but her body stiffened, quiet voice graduating into a growl. "He followed us."

"What? Who?"

"I can feel his darkness."
****

Joseph had no idea what she was talking about, but low level waves erupted from her, oozing over his skin, bringing a rash to the surface. It had been a very long time since he'd had goosebumps and he didn't like it.

She leapt from the vehicle and instead of heading toward the front entrance of the house, she darted back toward the street to scale the gate.

Joseph followed, tackling her before she could make the climb. They went down hard and he pressed the full weight of his body on hers, even as she snapped and growled.

"Stop, Dana."

She tried to wriggle free, her power vibrating through his teeth.

"Stop it!" He snarled in her ear. "You cannot kill someone in the middle of this neighborhood unless you want to be hunted down like some kind of dangerous animal. You will endanger all of us and I can't allow that."

Struggling, her growls thundered through her, but they slowed to subsiding when she couldn't escape. Despite the quiet, Joseph kept her pinned, mindful of her body beneath his and its disconcerting hum of power.

"Are you done?"

She didn't answer.

"Dana, I'm going to let you up, but you're not chasing your boogeyman. We're going to go up to the house where we both will be able to feed."

"Get off me."

Joseph debated, but when the vibration faded to a distant echo, he helped her to her feet, impressed when she didn't shake his hand off. Exhaustion deepened the lines already etched in her face, but he knew the remedy would erase it all. Her beauty would be restored and he looked forward to seeing it.

Keeping an arm around her despite her dirty look, they stepped up the path and rang the bell just to the right of the heavy double doors.

****

A slender woman wearing a red Asian-patterned silk robe answered. Bottle-induced flaxen hair and translucent green eyes belied the sharpness of her scrutiny. Music spread from behind her and where Dana would have expected Tchaikovsky or Mozart, what she got was The Carpenters. With a nod, the woman moved to the side to allow them entry. "Hello, Joseph. Please c'mon in. You're a little late tonight."

"Maggie. This is Dana." His arm kept her pinned to his side, just in case she decided to make another run for the gate, she figured.

The woman blinked at her gaunt countenance. "Looks like someone waited too long."

"Couldn't be helped." Joseph offered no explanation and Dana allowed a little gratitude toward him. She glanced over her shoulder into the night. Exhaustion had killed her temper, but the dark aura hadn't ceased to trouble her. It continued to pulse and shift outside the gate, an unfamiliar thunderhead on her periphery. Not the girl from the club and certainly not the same presence outside her window that night. A new threat. She didn't remember ever being this popular before and the grim thought almost brought a tiny humorless smile to her lips.

"Well, let's get that poor girl taken care of." The woman led them through an entry tiled with gleaming Travertine and into a side parlor with comfortable furniture, a shaggy area rug and a ménage a trois smack in the middle. A female vampire was drinking from the femoral artery of a well-built blond man while another man curled up around her lower half like a question mark and performed cunnilingus. The vampire didn't even bother to look up.

Dana stared, unsure she was seeing what she thought she was seeing. They seemed so comfortable and she felt her reality tip just a bit more into surreal with "Top of the World" playing in the background. David Soul followed the Carpenters a moment later and Dana blinked.

"Dana, this way." Joseph's hand pressed to her back, steering her past the spectacle and toward a small staircase on the other side of the room.

As she passed, the man performing oral duties looked up. He had long black hair tucked behind his ears and a Roman nose. "Want to join in, sweetheart?"

Startled, she didn't know how to react when Joseph gave a threatening belly growl that thundered throughout the room.

Fear flashing through his face, the man returned his attention to the vamp before him.

"You need to learn when to stop." Joseph spoke softly to her as they followed the blonde woman upstairs. "You'll feel the heart beating quickly in excitement, but when it starts to slow, you must stop feeding or you may kill him."

"These people ... sell their blood?" Among other things, apparently. Dana swallowed down some disgust.

"Yes, and they enjoy the privilege."

This was beyond sick, but the pain in her body kept her moving. The darkness outside had slid into secondary. "*Will* I be able to stop?"

"Yes. My blood should help with your control."

"Fortunately, Brandon is here tonight. Fledglings don't frighten him." Maggie stopped before one door of many and knocked with one knuckle. A deep voice from within acknowledged and she let herself in.

A boy in his early twenties twisted around to grin at them. He sat at a large desk just before the window, books, papers and a laptop spreading across the surface. Standing up, he was easily 6'3" and 210 pounds. Wavy black hair settled over his ears and friendly eyes the color of strong tea gazed out at them. Nodding at Joseph, he looked down at Dana, his smile still affixed. If her appearance disturbed him, he showed no sign. "Hi, I'm Brandon."

She glanced back at Joseph, who nodded, reassuring with his eyes before walking further up the hall with Maggie. Staring after him, she couldn't decide if she should run or not. All of it felt dirty somehow, like she was soliciting a prostitute.

"Are you okay?" Brandon ran a finger down her cheek, confident with youth and bravado. His touch felt hot, almost uncomfortable.

She didn't want to do this, but the hunger coiled in her belly and flickered outward, bringing shakiness and sickness. It hung over her, waiting for relief and if truth be told, the boy smelled amazing. The salt of his skin, the headiness of his blood, denseness of his muscles...

A tremor ran through her in anticipation.

Please let me not lose control.

He shut the door and turned back to her. "What artery do you prefer?"

God, this was weird. It was like being asked if she liked white or dark meat chicken. She didn't answer and looked up at him, curious. "How can you do this?"

His smile tilted up to the left and he shrugged.

"Why?"

The boy's face scrunched together and he appeared to contemplate. "Um, different reasons."

"Money."

"Yeah, but it's more than that. I mean, don't get me wrong, the money helps with school but..." He stopped, embarrassed.

He didn't need to continue. The kid got off on it and the thought made her feel sicker.

The burning inside flared and Dana closed her eyes, knowing she had to either make a choice or her instincts would make it for her. She could leave before feeding on this boy and do what? Play vigilante and track the dark aura outside? Kill someone in the middle of Queen Anne?

It might bring real estate prices down.

Dana tried not to let hysterical giggling overwhelm her again.

Brandon watched her, puzzled but expectant, with eyes dark with desire and excitement.

How long before her humanity would be gone? Would it be gone by tomorrow night? Next week? Would she notice when it happened? Isn't that the inevitability when you became a vampire? Or was that just fiction? She had no idea.

"Are you okay?" Brandon stepped closer, leaning down to brush his lips against her cheek. "Don't you want to do this? Aren't you hungry?"

She gazed at the throbbing on the side of his neck and the burning intensified. Moving like fluid, she pressed his face between her palms and stared up into his eyes. "Is it a walk on the wild side for you? Do you enjoy looking down into the precipice and thinking you're invincible? You do know you aren't, right?"

She could smell the sweat and fear well up on him and her hunger surged in response.

"This isn't my first time." His voice took on a defensive edge.

"I'm sure." Her fingers tightened slightly against his face. "How long before something bad happens, Brandon?"

"Why are you saying this to me? Nobody else does." It came out in a tiny whine and it reminded her how young he was. She wondered how his parents would feel about his curious extra-curricular activities.

"I'm not surprised, honey." Unable to hold back

any longer, she pulled him down to her and bit into the side of his throat. He gasped in surprise and pain and a moment later let out a satisfied sigh and grew hard against her.

Never would she have imagined something would taste so good. The best steak and seafood in the best restaurant couldn't even come close. His blood was pure as the strength of it flowed into and through her. She tasted youth, power and the invincibility she'd taunted him with. She sucked and swallowed greedily before remembering Joseph's warning.

The young man began to sag in her arms and she jerked her mouth away before his heart rate fell beyond the point of no return. Shame replaced the hunger.

She maneuvered the young man easily, his blood running through her in powerful waves and gently laid him on the bed. Curling up close, she brushed through his hair with her fingertips.

He cracked open his eyes a few minutes later and frowned.

"You all right?" Dana continued to stroke his hair and head. He was so soft. She thought of the time she'd touched a chinchilla and bit back a giggle. Everything was so unreal.

"Tired."

She'd taken too much and guilt flared, but at least he'd be okay. "I'll leave." She moved away, but he caught her hand in his.

"You don't have to or…" He squinted toward the window. "…or is it *that* time?"

There were still several hours until dawn, but she was ready to go. Not that she wanted to go back with Joseph, but for the moment she didn't have a lot of choices.

Not answering, Dana pulled a folded blanket

from the armchair next to the bed and tossed it over him. Brandon's smile relaxed as he dozed off. She figured the kid would sleep like a rock and recharge for next time.

She wondered if it was worth it to him.

Wandering to the window, she gazed into the partly overcast night, sensing *he* was still out there, waiting for … what? Whoever it was had followed them from her house, but it wouldn't happen again. Let Joseph take his fancy car home with him. She would leave on foot and disappear into nothingness. Maybe she couldn't take a life in the middle of an affluent neighborhood, but she could make tailing her impossible.

With Brandon's blood pumping through her, she felt strong, untouchable. No doubt a dangerous, arrogant feeling, but not untrue.

Passing by the narrow mirror affixed to the closet door, she paused, blinking in surprise.

She looked like *her* again. Her borrowed clothing made her look like a homeless waif, but the ghastly mask was gone. Trying out a smile, it felt a little uncomfortable, as if the muscles had rarely been used, but her canines weren't obvious.

Dana smiled again, throwing a little sideways smirk into it.

This time her new fangs gleamed through.

****

Mario kept several cars between them and he didn't see any indication he'd been spotted. Once they'd exited the highway, he'd had to be a little more discreet, but as usual, his everyman car called no attention.

He'd passed the house a few short moments after they'd pulled in through the gate and positioned himself in front of a neighbor's home with several newspapers in the driveway and no lights burning in the windows. It always amazed him how foolish some people could be. There may as well have been a neon sign in the window advertising the stately home was empty and "please burglarize at your own convenience."

Sheer stupidity.

Sighing, Mario hunkered down in his seat.

The ride over had given him time to analyze what he thought he'd seen and to toss it away as a trick of light, night, and cough syrup. He probably looked like a fool to Victor, but the only thing he could do about it was his job without any blunders.

Finishing his now lukewarm coffee, he tossed the Styrofoam cup on the floor, eyes straight ahead. He thought he'd noticed some kind of fuss behind the gate, but his angle was wrong to get a good look. There was no back entrance, so he just needed to bide his time to see where they headed next.

Using his phone, he tried to dig up some info on the house, but there was nothing to find. At least nothing easy. Come morning, he'd be able to do a little more digging or just pass it to Victor for further research. Mario hated that shit. He knew his boss would have some computer drone to take care of it.

Despite the leakiness of the head cold, he pulled a pack of smokes from the inside pocket of his jacket, lit up and pulled tar and nicotine deep inside his lungs. He also had a couple of joints, but figured the cough syrup had already done a number on his perceptions and he didn't need anything more to aggravate it.

Closing his eyes for a fraction of a moment, he cracked the window down and blew the noxious chemicals out into the clear night air. When he parted his lids, his body leapt and heart stopped for several very long moments.

The woman stood in the road less than ten yards in front of him. Her face didn't resemble the scary one his imagination had twisted into existence and, although his relief was palpable, new unease hastened his breath and blood pressure.

She didn't move, just stood there staring, hands hanging straight at her sides. Still dressed in those oversized clothes, she should have looked silly, but that wasn't even close to being the case. Something shimmered from her and there was no way he could put a finger on it. He just knew it couldn't be good.

With a slow hand, he reached for the Glock resting next to him on the passenger's seat. He wasn't supposed to take her out, but then again, circumstances changed and he doubted Victor would hold him responsible.

When he blinked, she was fifteen feet closer, her pale flesh capturing and holding the watery light from the moon for just a moment. His fingers curled around the grip, but he didn't lift the weapon, eyes unable to pull from the woman before him. Despite the rumpled hair and clothing, the lines of her face were exquisite and promised future wet dreams if he survived.

And then she smiled.

In that natural expression, Mario realized he was no longer a predator. The tables had shifted when he hadn't been looking and somehow he'd landed on the rung reserved for prey animals. There wasn't any time to completely digest the new information.

He screamed and hot urine soaked his jeans and upholstery when she rushed him. Instead of experiencing the agony of death, all he felt was the rocking of the car as she leapt onto the hood, sprang from the roof and disappeared from sight.

Chapter Fifteen

Alex closed his eyes and pinched the bridge of his nose. The last few hours had resulted in blurred vision and a thumping headache.

He'd taken a step to make himself useful. It was probably a pointless exercise, but it was something. He'd reached out to Joseph for any security camera footage, hoping the ones he'd noticed hadn't been dummies. The vampire had avoided answering his questions about Dana, but had willingly forwarded anything he had.

Not that it had mattered. He's gone over every bit of footage dozens of times and found nothing helpful. The club had been packed and singling out possible perpetrators was near impossible without Dana's input. It had just given him something to focus on until … what? Until he could stop reliving the past? Until he could muster a little bit of emotion toward himself that wasn't self-hate?

The morning after Dana's stabbing, he'd opted to take a leave of absence from work. His frame of mind left him worrying he'd make a wrong decision and get someone killed. His captain had stared at him from beneath deceptively heavy lids and nodded with a grunt, telling him he "looked like shit and to go get some rest for fuck's sake."

And now his feeble attempt to find her killer amounted from little to nothing.

When the landline rang, he ignored it. Only when he heard the gruff but familiar voice on the machine did he pause, hand frozen on the mouse in between pages.

"Alex, this is Sam Cleary. I hate to disturb you, but I was wondering if you've heard from Dana. She

didn't show for our weekly dinner tonight and, well, I know she gets involved in her projects, but it's not like her just to drop the ball like that. She doesn't answer at home or on her cell and I'm really getting worried. Give me a call back when you can."

"Shit." He figured he needed to stonewall, but had no idea how he should go about it. Dana was very close to her dad and brother, and there didn't seem a lot he could say that wouldn't sound like he pulled it out of his ass. If they were a couple, he could cite some kind of secret getaway or some such fable, but that wasn't the case. And Sam knew it.

Running a hand over his face, he gave it a couple of good scrubs. The need to seek her out was getting too strong for his own good. But then if she killed him, he wouldn't have to worry about running interference for his own selfishness.

Imaginary bugs crept and itched under his skin and he found himself pushing from the chair. He needed some air.

He slipped from his office, stopped to grab a bottle of beer from the fridge before flipping open the lock on the glass slider leading to his back deck. For more years than he cared to count, it had been his Zen spot where the tranquility of the woods and the steady current of the creek quieted his tendency to overthink.

Before he could cross the threshold, he faltered, the bottle of beer slipping from numb fingers.

Dana stood on the deck just inside the warm light emanating from the house, dark eyes watchful and unblinking. She was dressed in clothes too big for her and would have looked ridiculous before. Now nothing about her was ridiculous.

She stepped closer, movement smooth and graceful. She met his stare and Alex's heart rabbited as heavy emotions tangled into a mess of unresolved issues to line his stomach with acid. She was so beautiful, skin the creamy blushed porcelain of health. Some distant part of him became very aware that the leave he'd taken meant there would be no residual V-guard in his system. The only thing now protecting him was his lack of invite.

Alex couldn't pull his eyes away, knowing he should. Clearing his throat, he moistened his lips, but his words sounded as if they'd been rubbed raw by steel wool. "Should I be afraid of you?"

Tilting her head, she seemed to be weighing different answers to his simple question or just listening to some far away echo. "I can hear so much more now, Alex. You couldn't even imagine. Humans, so many of them, other animals, insects, fish. It should be overwhelming, but it's already starting to feel natural."

She hadn't answered his question, but he was helpless to move. Alex watched her, fascinated, every nuance familiar and at once, not.

"It's odd … I don't even know how to explain it to myself. I don't remember the *intense pain* of the headaches … or the relentless ache in my hip. I know it was there, I do, but the perception of it is gone." She met his eyes, looked away. "I'm not sure if that's the way it should be. It should be unnatural … but what *is* unnatural? Me? You'd think. But I shouldn't exist then, should I?"

"I don't know."

"I guess you wouldn't."

"I'm sorry, Dana."

"I…think *unnatural* might have a new meaning."
****

Alex continued to watch her, wary. She understood his reaction. Expected it. Everything was too crisp, new, somehow heavy at the same time. Maybe that was the world crushing her.

But now she had the strength to push back.

"I'm sorry I'm scaring you."

He didn't deny it, nor did he acknowledge it. "I thought I was going to lose you."

The simple admission stung. After her juvenile display outside Maggie's home, she hadn't had any kind of plan, but her subconscious had led her here. She could track his aura, but she could also detect his scent and emotions, just as she could with her father doing some night fishing on Lake Sammamish at this very moment or her brother tucking his boys in for the night. Raw pain struck an open nerve, but she stifled the emotion that surged, determined not to let all these new revelations unhinge her.

Now, as she gazed at Alex, she froze in indecision. He looked gaunt and exhausted, his face unshaven, eyes hollowed out by darkness. She knew him well, but still registered inward surprise that she could read his face so well. He'd always been practiced in stoicism, but now, she'd watched as a flicker of delight crossed him after his initial surprise, only to be overshadowed by sadness, fear and guilt.

Guilt.

He blamed himself, when the truth lay squarely on her shoulders.

They continued to stare at one another, but Alex's eyes shifted from hers, past her, back again and it occurred to her that he was afraid to get pulled in. That was okay. She couldn't really blame him for being cautious, but she expected it wouldn't matter if she decided she wanted him. A dark, unbidden thought, but one not untrue. "It's not your fault, you know."

Alex straightened and ran a hand through his hair. "That's not the way I see it."

"Were you planning on following me to the ladies' room? As good of friends as we are, that would have been crossing a line."

"I should have paid closer attention." He shoved his hands in the pockets of his jeans and stared at the floor of the deck just inches from his feet.

"You couldn't have known." His scent blossomed. His blood, skin and marrow washed over her and hunger took a sudden spike. She'd just fed. That couldn't be normal. Dana backed away from the circle of light.

"There's something I didn't tell you. I didn't want to ruin our evening because I knew how you'd react." She closed her eyes and shook her head. "It's not your fault. It's mine."

She could hear the softest slide of his boots when he moved closer. When she opened her eyes, he'd almost left the safety of the house. The push of two positive charges keeping her out was lost on him. If he extended the invitation or left the perimeter of his home, he would be vulnerable. "What are you talking about?"

"Don't come any closer, Alex. Please."

Stopping, he waited, while she told him about her late night visitor and its effect on her, both mentally and physically. "You would have taken extra precautions to be sure I was safe, if you had known. But the point's moot now."

Sighing, he reached over the threshold and touched her hand, weaving his fingers with hers. His flesh felt too hot and a tingle zapped up her arm. "With your record, I should have figured it was only a matter of time before there'd be some kind of backlash."

"You already had a car coming by the house several times a night."

"Not enough."

Staring down at their entwined digits, the hunger skewered her again and she stifled a groan. His heartbeat thudded in her ears, forcing warm and fragrant blood through his system, beckoning to her. An electrical charge merged them together and her fortitude wavered. "You're not safe. You need to step away."

"Dana." His thumb brushed the flesh of her palm.

"Back off!" She pulled her hand away and gave him a push as the air thickened around them.

Stumbling back, Alex knocked into the edge of his sofa, managing not to fall. Shock and fear stretched his features, while he stared at her, catching his breath. Sweat shone against his forehead.

"I'm sorry, Alex." Pain seared through her and she thought she felt the sting of tears, but the sensation dissipated. "I don't have … much control."

"What the hell was *that*?"

She didn't understand what he'd asked. What the hell was *what*?

Alex paused, changing his tact, seemingly dismissing whatever had disturbed him. "If I invited you in Dana, could you kill me?"

God, the way he smelled. Was it the emotional connection? "I'm not sure."

Frowning, she studied him. His eyes beseeched, guilt still bright within. He pulled at her, chipping away her semblance of control, sliver by sliver. He had every intention of allowing her within. She could sense it from that whirl of emotions residing deep inside.

It was time to go before he could do it. If that door opened, she didn't think she could resist the lure. She wasn't strong enough. Nausea rippled through her and a growing ache pressed against her heart.

"I have to go."

"Wait. Please." He stepped out onto the deck,

reaching out to her.

She shook her head, backing away before whirling and disappearing into the darkness.

****

Dana found herself downtown for lack of any other place to go, depression and anger twisting together in a volatile mix. Out of familiarity, she wandered near the entrance of Pike Place Market, stopping abruptly when she sensed and then saw the other vampire. He stood less than 30 feet from her, tall with gleaming silver hair, a long narrow nose and deep blue eyes. They gazed at one another, expressions blank. His brow gradually pinched into a frown and he cocked his head, not unlike an animal. A moment later he nodded to her.

The man was gone the next second and she blinked into the night.

Vampires blended. That's what she'd always been told. Not so much now. They existed on a different level of awareness now. Ethereal in appearance, an underlying viciousness lurked just below the surface. She wondered if she gave off the same vibration or if it would come with time.

Shaking her head, she banished the other vampire from her brain. He meant nothing. She had no idea of their numbers, but she couldn't—wouldn't—include herself with them.

Moving through the narrow streets, she watched for dark auras, figuring if she were going to snap, at least she wanted to take it out on someone who deserved it.

There was one across from the waterfront, under the viaduct. He thought he was hiding in the shadows as he squatted behind one of the pillars, pawing through a lady's handbag. It looked expensive and she wondered what became of its owner.

For a moment she found herself tempted, but the

hunger had dissipated. She'd fed well earlier and couldn't understand why it spiked again when she was with Alex. It didn't make sense.

She walked across the street, easily avoiding any passing traffic. There wasn't a lot open at this time, except for bars. Despite the size of the city, they rolled up the sidewalks at night. It was hardly New York. Wandering out onto the pier, she passed the Curiosity Shop with its mummies and assorted touristy treasures and continued to the end. Water lapped at the pilings and she watched the ebb and flow for what seemed like forever. The Ferris wheel loomed above her, a hulking structure skeletal in appearance, except for pods hanging like overripe fruit. At one time she'd loved the view it offered. Now nothing mattered. She'd been snatched away from everyone she cared about and the isolation was daunting.

"You need to find shelter, Dana." Joseph's voice murmured behind her.

His presence didn't surprise her. She'd felt him long before he spoke. It would unnerve her if she cared.

"Why? I'm not sure if I can ... *do this*." Any kind of survival instinct she may have had stretched to tearing. Or maybe she was just exhausted.

"It gets easier, believe it or not."

"How so? Easier to not care or easier to kill the people you love?"

He made a noise that would have been a sigh if he drew breath. "It becomes easier to control your cravings."

"It wasn't hard when I fed from Maggie's ... blood prostitute. But when I went to see Alex... I could barely control myself." She turned to face him, surprised to find the handsome face pinched with sadness. "Why *is* that?"

"Because there is no emotional bond with a *blood prostitute*." The term sounded tainted from his mouth.

She stared at him, considering his words. "So, if I bide my time, I could step back into my own life again? Or will everyone I care about be dead before I can learn control?"

"We need to go. Remember what I said."

Yeah, she remembered. 'Sunrise will drop you and you will die.'

The few stars peeking out from behind the cloud cover began to disappear as the night became lighter. Even with Joseph's car or a vampire's inherent speed, she didn't think there'd be time to find shelter anyway.

She gazed back toward the water and wondered how deep she'd have to go before the sunlight wouldn't reach her. How deep would be deep enough? Was it possible to just sit at the bottom of the ocean and wait for night to fall once again?

"Dana!" Joseph took her by the arm, but the moment she jerked out of his grasp, her knees buckled. He caught her before she hit the ground and they moved quickly. She wanted to fight off the arms around her, but her eyes filled with sand, sagging before everything blurred to darkness.

Chapter Sixteen

Dana once again awoke in unfamiliar surroundings, but these were choked with the smell of damp earth, rotten wood, rats, and garbage. Joseph was close, but she could also detect more of their kind beyond him, distant but there. She wondered if the silver haired vampire was amongst them and decided it was unlikely. He didn't look the type to sleep in filth.

Sitting up, Joseph's coat slid off her and she blinked at it in confusion before her eyes focused on her maker lying just a few feet away. He lay on his side, one hand flung outward, head tilted against the hard ground. Although new skin peeked from underneath, the right half of his face had been burned into charcoal and wet blisters. Dana gaped, shocked to witness the pinkness of healing push out the heinous injuries.

As she stared, he stirred and let out a pained groan. A moment later he returned her gaze and pushed himself into a sitting position. "Do I look that bad?"

"You're looking better every second."

Joseph smiled, but instead of charming, the effect twisted into ghastly. "Is that a compliment?"

She pushed herself away. "Not yet."

"In fairness, this wouldn't have happened if you hadn't chosen to play chicken with the sunrise." He pressed his lips together in a line of displeasure and his face rippled, new skin shimmering.

A twinge of guilt squeezed her insides. "I can't figure out how I even feel about this existence and yet you seem to be going above and beyond to protect me from myself. Why the hell would you do that?"

He touched his face with a shaking hand and

flinched. "I'm starting to wonder that myself. You're turning into a royal pain in the ass."

Frowning, she studied him more closely as something dawned. "How well do you know Alex?"

Joseph closed his eyes as pain coated his features. "Not well."

"How did you meet him?"

"If it's all the same to you, I have to regain my strength and feeding is the best way to do that." He tried to stand, faltered and sat back down. "Damn."

Dana rose and offered him her hand to help him up. Despite her ambivalence, she figured she owed him. If she wanted to be honest with herself, his suffering affected her on some baser plane that she really didn't care to analyze. "Where are we anyway?"

"Under the city."

It clicked after a moment and she nodded. The tunnels were what was left of old Seattle before the big fire of 1889 leveled it. They ran tours, but there were miles of catacombs sealed off from the general public. Not glamorous, but an effective hiding place if one stayed away from the skylights. "Where did you leave your fancy car?"

"You're not driving it."

Dana narrowed her eyes. "Seriously? You're worried about me driving your *car*? How the hell old are you anyway?"

"Old enough to remember gentility and yet respect the power of modern innovations."

"For God's sake." She helped him, sliding a hand around his waist when he stumbled. "Maybe I should just pick your pocket and not give you a choice. You don't have the strength to run, jump or whatever we do, and you probably can't drive either. Should I just stick you in a cab or something?"

He smirked, his face knitting together enough to make it less horrific. "Let's walk and see how things go."

Wariness drenched her, but far beneath, new excitement tingled through, confusion right behind it. "Walk and talk then. I still want to know how you know Alex."

"You're persistent. And nosy."

"One of my finer qualities." Hunger struck her like a fist and she doubled over. "Oh, God."

"We need to go. It's only going to get worse." Joseph threw an arm around her shoulders. "Normally it's harder on fledglings, but because of my ... damage, we're at the same level of need. It shouldn't be hard to hunt right now."

Hunt. "Can't we get to Maggie's?"

"I'm not sure. I guess we'll see what the night brings."

They hobbled toward the slight breeze of air wafting at them. Dana didn't have a clue where they were, in reference to the city, but she'd started to rely on instincts and trusted them not to lead her astray. Tours were usually a day thing and she didn't expect they'd stumble upon tourists and guides showing crumbling remains, the occasional quaint architectural detail and elevated commodes. The formal exit and entrance were based in a bar in Pioneer Square, if her memory was sound, but they couldn't very well pop up there after hours.

"This way." Joseph jerked his chin.

****

The streets were crowded in the early weekend night and people bumped into or narrowly avoided one another, but they didn't come near *them*. It was as if there was some kind of bubble around them humans felt uneasy entering. It was a little disturbing, but at the same time, a perpetual introvert, she found she liked it.

Joseph still wasn't capable of normal movement, so they kept mortal speed. This allowed her to examine human expressions even as they went out of their way to avoid her. Most didn't know, couldn't know, but something about the two of them seemed off, so the general populace swarmed around them, avoiding contact.

"You haven't answered my question, you know."

He gave her a side glance, lips pressing together for a moment before relenting. "A while back I entered a rather dark place. Because of this, more by accident than anything, Alexander saved my life."

Raising her brows, she fixed him with a curious stare, waiting.

"If you want to know more, ask *him*." His tone indicated finality and she chose not to push. Yet.

They left the crowds behind by slipping down a side alley to head toward the parking garage. He didn't want to leave his vehicle behind and Dana found this profoundly amusing. Male was male, whether vampire or human.

The mingled scent hit them both at the same time and they swiveled.

Two humans moved toward them, attempting stealth. Dana's keen eyes cut through the night and she could see their dark auras twisting around them.

She'd passed on prey the evening before, but her stomach now rolled in anticipation. This was too good to be true and her hunger leapt as if a separate animal. She glanced at Joseph in time to see him lick his lips and his eyes go completely black. Her own appearance must have been similar and a predator's instinct rushed her, bringing pleasure and a ghost of fear.

Their would-be muggers were going to be in for a

treat, even as they split to cut their quarry off. Dana fought not to laugh out loud. *What the hell is the matter with me?* The thought slid away the moment before it could take root.

When they passed the dumpster, one stepped out from behind it while the other appeared in front of them.

There was the flash of steel and a grunted demand of "wallet" directed at Joseph.

The top layer of dirt and grime didn't smell very good to Dana, but underneath she expected would be wonderful. Or at least appeasing.

Joseph said nothing, but he did smile. When the man stepped closer to press his point with a wave of his little pistol, his expression faltered at the same moment her maker grabbed him. The gun clattered to the asphalt and slid under the dumpster.

"Fuck!" The one behind them pivoted to take off, but Dana caught him by the hair, jerked him off his feet and flat onto his back. She covered his mouth with one hand as he began to squeal.

"Nuh uh. None of that." Her voice gentled, became even demure and she smiled. He thrashed, but the panic left him almost immediately as he sighed and relaxed. It was good, not great, but still his blood satiated the physical hunger. She stopped feeding when his heart rate began to dip, but Joseph's voice reached her ears.

"You may as well finish, Dana. We will need to dispose of them."

She looked up to see blood on Joseph's lips and his face healed. He grinned at her and she almost grinned back. Unnerved, but oddly turned on at the same time, she found herself disturbed by that realization.

The man lying next to her was unconscious and pale. It wouldn't take much.

There was a low snap and she glanced back over

just after Joseph broke the other man's neck. The grin had gone and he was all business, as if dumping the garbage.

Horror at the implications struck her and she fell backward to scramble away. She considered throwing up, but didn't want to lose her meal. The hunger would be so much worse.

"I'm sorry. It's just something that needs to be done."

Maybe her humanity wasn't gone. As different as she'd become, she couldn't bring herself to end the man's life. "I can't."

Joseph appeared at her side and she didn't move away, but she didn't move closer either. "You learn to protect yourself. This is how many vampires hunt. Of course, some are far less discriminating."

"How often do *you* ... hunt ... this way?"

His slender fingers squeezed her chin and he made her meet his eyes. They weren't black any longer. They were back to lovely flecks of brown, gold and green. "Not as much as you might think."

She wanted to believe him, but couldn't. The blood on his lips, the delighted grin and the snapping of the neck sickened her. Disgusted, she shrank from his touch, shaking her head, a low moan escaping before she could stop it.

"You need to finish, Dana." He became insistent. "If you leave him like this, humans will hunt us."

"I can't."

"You can. It'll be quick and painless."

"How can you know that?" She trembled and wanted to cry in frustration at how unfair everything had now become.

Face still, he watched as she pushed further away. With one quick motion, he took the man's chin in one hand and jerked it around with a crunching sound.

Recoiling again, she rolled to her feet to put as much distance between them as she could. Some part understood, but the rest remained in denial over what she'd become. It was difficult enough to come to terms with being a vampire, but even harder to accept she was now a killer, even if not in practice yet. Would it be inevitable or would she be able to walk that fine line?

She couldn't just turn into some nighttime predator randomly disposing of lives. That was unacceptable. She needed to somehow hold onto whatever made her, her. Strength had been something she'd had from the time she was young and lost her mother, up to losing Jesse. It *had* to serve her now. She'd make it.

Despite her horror and growing anger, she waffled on doing what she shouldn't. It was because of Joseph that she walked the tightrope between midnight and light, but she was terrified it would only take a nudge to send her into darkness. She needed an anchor in her old world. A touchstone she'd run from the previous night.

Making a quick decision, she decided to feed again to make sure her hunger didn't rear up and then go see Alex. Maybe she was an idiot, but she needed him.

****

Victor sat across from a jeans-clad, gangly man with a bushy auburn beard highlighted with traces of black and grey. The same fur-like hair sprouted in unruly eyebrows and crested in a tumbleweed sprouting from his skull. Leathery skin poked from around all the fuzz and denim, except where patches of smooth burn scars gave the flesh of the man's hand, throat, and leftover nub of an ear a shiny, reptilian look Victor strained to keep from returning to. Keen brown eyes cut through the hair and disfigurement, sizing him up even as he did the same.

Loud rockabilly and the buzz saw of hundreds of human voices converged to allow privacy for the two men. The server had stopped at the booth twice and wouldn't again until summoned.

Victor took a pull of his porter, noting with some distaste, that the other man's choice ran to piss-water beer. But then again, he shouldn't have been surprised.

"So, you need to outsource, huh?" Thadeus Baker's voice growled through smoker's lungs and the scarring that touched his throat.

"That's one way to look at it. I understand you're the person to see about such matters."

Baker grunted and downed half his piss-water in two gulps. "I can be. Risky business, though."

"So it would seem." Victor made eye contact, but kept his face impassive.

"You told my associate it's a fledgling."

"Yes."

"Usually makes it easier. They're not as strong." He took another gulp, thin foam touching the corner of his mouth. "Unless of course, the sire is lurking about and feeling protective."

"Is that the norm?" Victor tilted his head, genuinely curious.

The man shifted, the wood of the bench seat creaking. "Only happened once, but—" He waved a long-fingered hand in front of his face. "It was almost my last hunt. Was in the hospital for months. Ever have skin grafting?"

At Victor's wordless head shake, Baker nodded. "I don't recommend it."

"Am I wasting my time with this meeting then?" Annoyance leaked into his composure. If this man wasn't prepared to deal with the repercussions of his chosen profession, Victor needed to find someone who was. Caras had begun to make the noise of a spoiled child and he didn't want to hear it. He doubted the Greek had any clue how off putting the tantrums were. "If you're not as good as I've heard or you've lost your taste for it, I need to find someone else then."

"Hold on, Mr. Alvarez. I didn't say I wasn't interested. I was just pointing out some of the risks, so you understand my fee." The tall man pressed his hands flat against the table, eyes glinting, brows quirking upward.

"I don't care about your fee. My personal experience does not run to this kind of job. Frankly it would be easier for all concerned if it did, but that's not the case, so I need to 'outsource' as you so eloquently put it. Now that that's out there, let it be known that I intend to stay involved in this situation."

A smile showed nicotine stained teeth. "You looking to pick up some experience?"

"Let's just say I'm a very curious man."

Baker stared at him, pursing his lips for a moment before shrugging. "Sure. Your funeral if things go bad. Now that we have an understanding, do you have a picture of it?"

Frowning at the man's reference to Dana Chambers as an 'it,' he reached into the inner pocket of his coat for the simple manila envelope and slid it across the table.

With blunt-tipped fingers, Baker pulled out the three photos they'd managed to attain and his eyes widened. "Well, isn't that a damned shame? It's good-looking."

Good-looking didn't come close to describing the woman. Victor considered himself quite the connoisseur of both wine and women, not counting his playthings, of course. With her porcelain features and dark, shiny hair, the word he would have used was 'beautiful' or perhaps 'stunning,' but this hick probably looked at females only in terms of seminal receptacles. One thing the man said did smell of truth though. It *was* a damned shame.

"Who's this guy?" Baker tapped one photo.

"Alexander Kelly. Her partner, professionally, and possibly personally."

He made a noise, deep and phlegmy in his throat. "Good to know. Could come in handy."

Chapter Seventeen

Dana's appearance had shaken him, but hadn't lessened the emotions burgeoning within. He needed to channel his thoughts, energies. If he found those responsible, he might be able to ease his conscience at the very least or even prevent another attempt. Vampires weren't invulnerable and there were folks out there who were aware of it.

Pursuing another possibility, he researched past collars Dana had had a hand in putting away. The majority of them were sitting pretty much right where they were supposed to be, but he came across old information that had spilt over his desk months before. At the time he'd filed it under "No longer a waste of oxygen," but now, he peered at the computer screen, hackles rising and stomach twisting. Alex remembered the guy all too well.

Gabriel Petros had been a 26-year-old rapist and sadist and he'd also had the distinction of being the first hunt to make Dana physically ill. During a transfer from county, an irate father took him out in a spray of buckshot, wounding one deputy and coating the other with gore. He'd been survived by his mother, Lily, father dead, no siblings.

Curious, Alex dug a little more on mama. 53 years old, widowed since 1996 when the husband dropped dead from an embolism, nice condo in the Capitol Hill area of the city, no listing of occupation. Her parents deceased, one brother, a Charles Caras.

The worn leather chair creaked in protest when Alex leaned back.

Charles Caras.

Where had he heard that name before?

Reaching out, Alex tapped a few more keys, quickly scanning information. The guy made most of his money in shipping ... okay, that's what it was. Several years back the DEA had been investigating him, but the case had landed egg on their face, when incriminating evidence had mysteriously disappeared along with their star witness. Another dirty rich guy able to cover his tracks.

A rich guy with a dead nephew and mourning sister.

Possible connection?

Maybe, but the odds weren't great.

He pressed on. Another possibility caught his attention. Trenton Dimas. Had a thing for beating up prostitutes and cutting off their eyelids. Pulled serious time before somehow making parole. A week later he mixed it up with an old girlfriend and honed his craft all over her. Dana helped track him to an old warehouse on the south side. Alex seemed to remember an irate brother claiming a frame job.

Tapping a few keys, he brought up an image of Carl Dimas. Pock-marked, heavy faced, with rolls of flesh where a neck should have been. Still in the city. Possible.

And then there was the very last hunt. Billy Hayes. The devil with the baby face.

Rubbing his eyes, Alex pushed from the chair to leave his office in search of a beer. For the most fleeting of moments, he contemplated something stronger, but dismissed the impulse in irritation. Grabbing a bottle, he popped the top, took a swig and started to return to his desk, halting at the strong knock at the door.

Placing the bottle on the counter, he crossed to the foyer, aware of his .38 now nestled within the drawer of the end table, but choosing not to pull it out. More than likely it would be the elderly neighbor from the next property asking him to investigate some weird noise or shadow. It wouldn't be the first time.

When he unlocked the deadbolt and pulled the door open, he inwardly sighed. Dana's father stood, trying to glare at him from the doorstep. Sam Cleary was a big burly guy with wavy iron-gray hair and intense eyes. Normally confident, worry had shredded his demeanor into a shadow and the glare failed. He balled up his meaty hands and shoved them into the pockets of his coat. "Alex."

"Sam. I didn't expect you to come by."

"Of course you wouldn't. If you had bothered to return my calls, I wouldn't be standing here right now." The man stopped, eyed him and frowned. "You look like shit."

Alex almost smiled. Irritated and caustic was much better than fearful. "Thanks. I can always count on you for your brutal honesty."

The man waved a hand. "Normally, I'd be annoyed at having to drive over this way, but I'm looking for my daughter. She missed dinner last night, no calls, nothing and Bokken's still with me. Andy hasn't heard from her either. This just isn't *like* her." His eyes passed Alex and into the house, as if expecting to find his daughter hiding under the couch or possibly on a bookshelf filed under "D." "Seems like you two are always together so I thought I'd check in here before I haul myself all the way out to her place."

****

A soft sigh had both men shifting and Dana appeared behind them on the doorstep. "I'm sorry, Dad. I didn't mean to worry you. I just had a client that insisted on meeting in person. I had to go to California. It was a spur of the moment kind of thing."

Wide relief spread across her father's broad features and deep unease settled into Alex's. He took a tiny step back and the movement saddened, but didn't surprise, her.

She'd hesitated when she'd recognized her father's vehicle in Alex's driveway, but wasn't exactly shocked to find him looking for her. The timing could have been better, though. Having fed, she knew she looked human and she could only hope it would continue. Something wild lurked deep inside with the potential of revealing itself at inopportune moments. The possibility made fear curdle in her stomach like old milk. Hiding her thoughts, she turned a bright smile on them.

"You had me scared to death! What's with this no-show, no-call business?" Fear whooshed away and relief buckled over into aggravation. Her dad was ready to give it to her on the chin for her thoughtlessness. "A *job* had you forgetting your responsibilities to your family? Dana, that's not like you."

"I'm sorry. I just got caught up. It's a great opportunity." She tilted her head as she lied and looked up into her father's eyes. Remorse flared with the keen edge of a knife blade. "I'll try not to let it happen again. You know I prefer to stay close to home."

Aware of Alex's frown, she kept her gaze locked, watching as her father's stern expression washed away in a puzzled smile. "Do me a favor, though?"

"Sure, Dad."

"Call your brother. He's been worried, too."

"Will do. You guys are both such huge worry warts." She wanted to step closer, but the push from the threshold had her teetering on her heels.

"Is there any reason you're standing outside, Dana? You can come in you know." Alex said softly, not allowing any other emotion to intrude even as the protection of his home evaporated around him.

Too aware of the ramifications, Dana offered him the best smile she could muster before stepping inside and going up on her toes to give her father's cheek a peck. "I'll give you a call later, okay? I really need to speak with Alex right now."

Sam blinked, but continued to smile. "That's okay. I should get going anyway. Fishing early tomorrow."

"Didn't you just go out?"

His brows drew down. "Yeah, but how did you know?"

Dana shrugged, nonplussed. "You *always* go out. I'll see you soon. Love you, Dad."

"When are you picking up your dog?'

She hesitated. "Soon."

Tension cut through her when her father pulled her into a bear hug. A moment later he held her at arm's length, a frown creasing his face. "Sure you're okay? You seem kind of off."

"Fine. Just tired."

"If you're sure." He released her and nodded to the younger man. "Good night, Alex."

"Night, Sam."

Solace hung over him, radiating outward. He pressed a kiss to the top of Dana's head before stepping past Alex and back into the night. They both watched him follow the short path to the driveway before climbing into his SUV and pulling away. Alex closed the door, hesitated, but locked it anyway.

Dana stared down at the carpet, shame trying to push out tears, but not succeeding. "I can't believe I just did that to my own father."

"It was intentional then."

She gazed up at him, noting the heavy fatigue etched in his handsome face. "Yeah, that time it was. I just didn't want him to worry ... or question. I'm confused enough without trying to explain anything to my family."

Pausing, she looked past him, not bothering with stoicism now, control cracking apart. "I'm sorry about ... last time. I'm just having a hard time with this. I don't know *how* to be this way."

"Understandable." Glancing away, he concentrated somewhere beyond the room, possibly beyond the new reality.

She gazed at him, feeling his guilt. Feeling his fear.

"Why did you invite me?"

"How could I not?"

Anguish leaked from his words and she closed her eyes for a moment, sensing the whirlwind of emotions near to bursting from him. She took a step closer, relieved when he didn't back away. "Tell me what happened that night."

He scraped his hand through his hair, a deep breath shuddering from him. "What do you want me to say, Dana? That you were dying? That I'm so fucking self-centered because I couldn't stand the thought of it? Whatever happens at this point, it's not like I don't have it coming."

Realizing the meaning beyond the words, she reached out and trailed her fingertips across his unshaven cheek, the pinpricks of his beard contrasting with his soft flesh. The aroma of his blood washed over her, even as the sound of it pumping through his system pressed into her ears. "Did you personally change me, Alex?"

His brow furrowed. The question was rhetorical so he said nothing.

"Then why do you blame yourself? Did you ask? Did Joseph offer out of the kindness of his heart?"

Licking his dry lips, he stared beyond her. "Both, I guess, although I doubt any kindness on Joseph's behalf entered the equation."

"You promised Jesse you'd look after me and would have failed if I had died."

"Jesse has nothing to do with it. It's on me. I couldn't stand the idea of losing you, so I took Joseph up on the offer." He dropped his eyes to the floor, even as her cool hand pressed against his face.

"He owed you a favor."

Not responding, his gaze remained glued to another part of the room.

The grandfather clock Alex had inherited from his uncle chimed the half hour, but internal quiet flooded between them. Neither moved.

"You know what I was thinking earlier *that* night?" She finally murmured, stepping close enough to brush against him, seeing his shudder and how he still didn't try to back away. Hunger reared up inside, but it seemed different, more emotional, less physical. For better or worse, it was what brought her here tonight.

"What?"

She moved her hands over his chest, up to his shoulders, enjoying the feel of his solid body beneath her palms. The scent of him clung to her nose, his blood, yes, but also the faint aroma of beer on his breath, the soap and deodorant of his morning routine, the salty-savory sweetness of his flesh. "I was thinking I might take you into my bed."

His breath stopped, held, and resumed. The muscles beneath her touch hardened in tension.

"I told you I don't know how to be like this, but you're my link to who I was, who I want to remain. I don't want to lose myself. Please." Control wavering, she stretched up and kissed the corner of his mouth. "Don't be afraid."

What should have been obvious *before* now wove around her in a warm and comforting hug. Alex loved her. She could feel it shimmer off him in waves, rushing at her with a gentle homecoming. Dana could only wish her own feelings were as easy to identify now. She knew her draw to him was powerful, but couldn't distinguish between the physical and the emotional. He'd been her rock as a mortal and now as she drifted in an unfamiliar realm, she needed him as an anchor as an immortal. So fearful of losing her humanity, she was willing to use this wonderful man in the worst way possible.

Dana tilted her head, she wondered how he'd taste. Not like Joseph. Like one of Maggie's boys? He was older than most of them by a good ten years. Does age affect it? Maybe. Probably lots of different factors affect their flavor. Alex took care of himself. He ate well, limited the crap intake, allowing Red Mill or XXX Burgers only once or twice a month. He ran, boxed at the gym. His blood would be superb she had little doubt. She smoothed one hand down the side of his throat, fingers trailing over his pulse thrumming wildly under her touch. His scent invaded every part of her. She could smell his fear, but also his excitement. Was it because of who she was or who she used to be?

Alex's vivid eyes connected with hers as he touched her face. She could sense him starting to go under and wondered if she'd ever have any control of it. Sifting her fingers into his hair, she brought him down to her to meld her mouth with his.

He slid his arms around her waist to bring her flush against him. His lips and tongue slowly perused hers, warm and gentle. This was what he'd wanted. He wore it as openly as his own skin. His tenderness resonated deep inside and her eyes stung.

But it wasn't enough. Something wild licked at her insides. Something dark, waiting to be unleashed. Something not her.

With little thought of her new strength, she shoved him into the wall to surround him, sink into him, instinctively blocking any escape he might choose. Dana froze when his breath whooshed out of him in a torrent. Dark horror and realization threaded through her. "Oh, Alex, I'm sorry."

Recovering quickly, he caught her by the shoulders and shook his head. Hesitating one spare moment, he yanked her close to cover her mouth with his. A low growl of need escaped him as he elevated the kiss, shooting bolts of excitement throughout her body.

The connection of dark and light, love and lust, and a primal instinct larger than both of them, fused their bodies together, the kiss quickly shifting from tentative and tender into animalistic excitement. His arms entwined around her, as they clashed with teeth, fangs, lips and frenetic tongues. Framing his face with her fingers, she held him to her, closing her eyes as his hands ran over her back and hips, pressing, stroking, eliciting tingles.

"Is ... this ... a good idea?" His breath heated her cheek and he nipped her earlobe.

It was a terrible idea, but her body trembled and pulsated in anticipation and blinding lust. Not answering, she pressed her lips hard to his, even as he swept her into his arms and took her upstairs.

They got as far as the hallway before she skipped the buttons to rip his shirt open and claw his chest. Allowing her to her feet, he yanked her blouse over her head, dropping it and unhooking her bra as they staggered toward his bedroom. Unencumbered, Alex pressed his mouth to her neck and shoulders, shuddering and tensing when she did the same. He probably expected blood to flow and she didn't know how long she could refrain from accommodating him.

Everything blurred and her past disappeared as her new animal bolted forward. She wanted him in every sense of the word and exhilaration swept through her, a cool rush of pleasure. Her fingers pulled at the fly of his jeans and they fell into the soft down of his comforter, hands grappling, clothing shredding, dropping or disappearing.

Blood rushed just beneath the surface of those wonderful, lean muscles, beckoning with a richness she could smell. She sunk her fangs into this throat when he drove into her, his gasp of surprise not keeping him from thrusting deeply, rhythmically, angling for her pleasure. His flavor was a lush blend of tangy, sweet and savory and with some regret she released her fangs and pressed soft lips to his cheeks and lips instead, pushing her hips up to meet his frenzied movement. His aura, the same blue as his eyes snaked around them, merging them into one being, one connection.

Darkness flickered with flashes of light behind her eyes as her body coiled, held firm for several agonizing seconds before exploding into thousands of stars. Her muscles pulsed and clamped down on him in a forceful vise and Alex's eyes widened in surprise and borderline pain, but he didn't falter.

Too bright. Too much. Her senses screamed unfamiliar, blade-sharp, overwhelming. Too aware. Flesh, sweat, the act of making love brilliant, luminous, blinding. Sensations rose through and above her skin.

With a hoarse scream, she flipped around so she could look down upon him, her hair brushing his face, staring into those magnificent eyes of his, watching them soften in contact with hers. Alex pressed her close and she groaned when he sucked the tip of her breast into his mouth, swirling his tongue around it to a stiff peak. His hands caressed her back, kneaded her butt and then returned to thread in her hair and drag her lips back down to his, firm and possessive. She pressed another kiss to his lower lip before pulling away to piston upon him, his hardness filling her, threatening more explosions in the darkness.

Her mind going blank, whirls of sensation crowded inside and pushed her toward the steep cliff she hadn't climbed in a very long time. She wasn't sure about the vampire part of her, but the woman who so wanted to keep a toehold in humanity shuddered and gasped as two more climaxes shot through her in succession. Bursts of color wavered in her vision as she weakened. Grabbing his sweat-slicked shoulders to keep upright, she collapsed forward anyway. Stiffening beneath, Alex spent himself with a guttural cry, his body trembling even as his breath rasped against her cheek.

Reaching for her, he tucked her down against him and she let him, turning into a puddle within the crook of his arm and chest, while he pressed kisses to her head and brow. Stroking the firmness of his flesh, exhaustion turned her control to mist. Without thought, Dana slid up and buried her fangs in his throat a second time.

Alex grunted, but made no attempt to push her away. His lovely flavor filled her senses once more and she swallowed deep, smooth and lustful, while his hand stroked her hair. She jerked away moments later when her mind snapped back and his gentle caresses fell away. Pain and guilt shredded through her.

"I'm sorry." Staring up at him, worry stirred from deep within when he turned his head to cast heavy eyes on her from a pale face. "I shouldn't... I couldn't stop..."

"It's okay. I know you couldn't help it..." He blinked, slow and sleepy, a trace of curiosity sliding in. "You didn't...?"

Dana shook her head. "No, I don't think so."

"All right then..." His eyes sunk shut before one popped back open to regard her. "How do I taste?"

Incredulous, she smiled at him. "You're serious?"

"Mm hm."

Dana squirmed up to kiss his jaw. "Delicious."

"Good to know."

He dozed off and she watched him, eyes peeling away the darkness like a new day. She could see every whisker, fine line, pore, scar and texture of every hair. Under a microscope everyone should suffer, but Alex didn't. She could keep looking at him forever. Emotions stirred and her eyes moistened for the first time, amusement at their exchange gone. Would the rashness of this act haunt them both? There was no way to know. A single tear crested on her nose and dropped onto his chest.

Glancing out at the night sky, she wavered. She wanted to stay close just a little longer, knowing she'd want to make love again, unsure if she should allow it. Horror blossomed within her as she watched welts and bruises appear on his flesh. The raised pink swell of nail marks stood against his chest, while a swirl of purple and black touched his hips, smearing up to his ribcage where her legs had locked around him. She could only imagine what his back looked like. Had she *really* done all that?

Bite marks left by her razor fangs were no longer bleeding, eliciting a shiver deep inside. She hadn't changed him ... had she? Had she lied? No, bruises wouldn't be forming if that were the case. There must be something in *her* that promotes healing. Dana almost laughed at the irony.

The thought of laughter died before it could be realized and a dark empty chasm of depression spread under her and beckoned.

She'd *hurt* him. What if she'd broken bones or ruptured organs? Was he really sleeping or had he lost consciousness from internal injuries?

Nausea settled heavy inside as pinpricks of sweat stood against her skin. With gentle fingers she pushed spikes of hair off his brow, hesitated, before checking for a weak or erratic pulse.

"Can't feel my legs," he murmured.

She blinked, sickness swelling into the back of her throat. "*What?*"

Cracking his eyes open, he stared at her for several long seconds before a slow smile curved the corner of his mouth.

Gaping, her brows furrowed and the urge to bite him again surged. His playful response threw her and she couldn't hold back a smile. "That was low."

"Mm hm."

"You're a jerk."

"I know." He didn't move, just fixed his gaze to the left of her eyes. "Not dead though. Not yet, at least."

Relief closed the chasm for the moment and she kissed him, gentle with a little more mindfulness of her own strength. "I didn't mean to…"

"Shhh, it's okay." A teasing light filled his eyes. "Admittedly, I'd hoped … if we even got to this point … that our first time would be a little more … tender, but this was … *interesting*…"

Dana studied him, wondering if he was delusional. "Interesting?"

"But exciting."

She focused on the tone of his voice and the

emotions she could feel reverberating from him, not the bruises coating his body. "Not afraid any longer?"

"Of course I am. I'm not a complete moron." He swallowed, colliding with her eyes once more. "I just care too damn much about you to let it get in the way."

Settling down against him, she stroked her fingertips across his skin, noting her unsteady hands, but happy for the moment of levity in her newly twisted existence. "You're a foolhardy man."

"Yeah, I know." He kissed the top of her head, bringing his hand up to brush through her hair. "Doubtful I could change now."

"Probably not, but one can hope."

"Attack me and *then* insult me," he muttered.

Her gaze touched every part of his face, a warm glow inside burning a little brighter only to snuff out when she noticed the bite marks she'd left on them.

They were healing so quickly. Scabs were forming.

Inclining his head, he smiled down at her with loving acceptance in his eyes. Acceptance. He didn't care what she now was.

Push. Pull. Push. Pull.

Stretching up, she lightly ran her lips across his cheek before darting her tongue out to touch his earlobe with a quick swipe, trying to lure, unsure if he even had the energy.

A moan vibrated in his chest and he pulled her into a kiss, his mouth warm and soft.

To avoid hurting him, she gave herself up to let him set the pace, shuddering and arching beneath his fingertips as they explored and caressed, his lips setting her soul alight and making her forget everything. The slide of his body against hers, the rhythm of strokes and the tingling crescendo of sensation sent her over the edge in waves of heat and pleasure.

Afterward, she watched him sleep in earnest, the rise and fall of his chest comforting, the sound of his steady breathing a reminder of how gloriously alive he was. Dana curled into him, resting her head upon his shoulder and savoring a few more stolen moments before necessity would force her away from him and back into the darkness.

Day and night would always separate them now. She'd never be able to look up at him and see the sunlight casting a dozen different hues of gold in his hair or how, on a clear day, the sky would match the shimmering bright blue of his eyes.

Reluctant tears broke free to slide down her face to land on Alex in silence.

Chapter Eighteen

She headed for the underground and Joseph had every intention of catching her before she settled among the broken beams, dust and vermin.

It was undignified. Vampires weren't animals scratching at some semblance of existence and he didn't want his fledgling behaving as such. Not to say there weren't times when going beneath the surface wasn't necessary. Throughout his lifespan he'd found himself in caves, cellars or just in hastily dug out holes, but such experiences were never the rule and he didn't want them to be for Dana. They stood at the top of the food chain and should behave as such.

He found her walking past the totem at Pioneer Square, but stopped short before reaching out. Moving slower than mortal, her emotions twisted in confusion and violence, eliciting that strange vibration of power which alternately frightened and intrigued him. But that wasn't what made him pause. It was her smell.

She'd been with Alexander.

He should have expected it. Emotions ran deep and unwavering between the two of them, but Joseph couldn't help but wonder whether or not Alexander survived the experience. Most didn't.

"Are you following me again?" Her sullen voice whispered through the quiet pre-dawn hour.

"I don't need to follow you. I can always feel your presence." He fell in step with her, not reacting to the tightening of her mouth. "I assume you're going underground?"

She kept moving in the direction of the alley.

"You don't have to do that. My home is much

more comfortable."

"I don't think that's a good idea." She stopped several yards away, eyeing the hidden entrance to the broken world below the city.

"Why? Because it would feel like a betrayal to Alexander?"

Dana turned on foot and glared at him.

"I take it he's still alive?"

"Of course." Annoyed, the word came out in a growl and Joseph almost smiled. She had much more control than most fledglings and he felt a stirring of pride. He wondered how many times she'd fed from the man. It wasn't a good idea to continue to return to one source for nourishment. That's why Maggie shifted her clients and employees around. It avoided possible complications.

The stench of human refuse, urine, dust and ancient death rose around them from the alley and below. Dana stared ahead, unmoving.

Joseph waited, running a careful gaze over her lovely face, detecting the subtle tracks of dried tears against her cheeks. Startled, he narrowed his eyes, expecting they were playing tricks of fatigue and a long night. Crying wasn't something he was capable of. He'd never even met another vampire who was. Compassion hooked within and he spoke gently. "I'm sorry the transition is so difficult. I do promise it'll get better."

She said nothing.

"Do you honestly like sleeping with the rats?" He stared at the manhole cover leading to emergency sanctuary, trying not to curl a lip.

"Yes, I do. Actually, it's in my top ten all-time favorite things to experience." Dana turned toward him, expression lost and struggling, but a glint of sardonic humor seeping through.

Joseph stared at her for a moment before smiling and shaking his head. "My home remains open to you. It is a place to sleep, nothing more. We only have an hour or so for you to decide though."

Peering down the alley, she wrinkled her nose in disgust. Her dark eyes darted to find his and she stared at him for several long moment before resignation seeped in. "Will you tell me what happened between you and Alex?"

"I gather there wasn't time or *opportunity* to ask *him*?"

She scowled at him, her indignance bringing a smile to his lips. "That's none of your business."

Joseph shrugged, amused despite her annoyance.

With one last glance toward the underground, she seemed to resign herself, nodding a moment later. "Fine."

****

His two-story prairie-style home was nestled on a deep lot boasting numerous mature evergreens for privacy. Although well-maintained, it didn't go above and beyond to catch the eye and Dana figured that was a deliberate move on Joseph's part.

The first floor was an exercise in modern with clean lines and a cold, uninviting feel. As far as Dana could tell, the spartan and uninspired furniture must have been lined up in precision with a protractor. With the exception of one insipid watercolor print above the unused fireplace, the walls were bare. It could have been a model home without any attempt at hominess.

She didn't even try to hide her underwhelmed reaction and Joseph smiled. "This way."

He led her through the bland interior, including a dining room with a cheap, simple Quaker table and chair set and an untouched kitchen. Just beyond the brushed steel refrigerator, he pulled open a pantry door and waved her inside. The metal shelving was bare, with the exception of a few standard cleaning products. Another door waited at the far end. Stepping close to her, he reached over to disengage three heavy duty locks before pushing in and flipping on the overhead lights.

A plush, carpeted stairway led down and angled out of sight.

Dana hesitated, but Joseph's amused and patient expression had her moving down the steps before him. Stopping on the second landing, she stared below her, mouth agape at his basement sanctum.

It could have been a historian's wet dream.

The main room was awash in items from dozens of different eras. A curved mohair sofa dominated the space, but every other nook and cranny was filled. She wasn't the most educated in antiques, but through personal interest, managed to recognize several items including the old Edison home phonograph, a film projector from the 20's, a Civil War bayonet, a stereo console from the 1960's, a mid-20th century slot machine and what appeared to be a 19th century Louis-Philippe cabinet hiding under several boxes of who-knew-what. She turned to gape at Joseph. "How old *are* you?"

"Let me show you where you can sleep." He cast a glance at her from the corner of his eye as he led her down a narrow hallway splitting off from the main room. "In answer to your question, I suppose I have two birthdays. The first would be January 4, 1746 and the second, April 17, 1781."

"I guess cake and party favors are blasé at this point," she muttered, reeling at the enormity of it all. At 29, thanks to genetics, she held onto the face of someone a decade younger. Now she would remain as she was. When Alex was 80, she'd *still* be 29, with the face of a teenager. A wave of dizziness swept through her and she reached out to touch the wall for support. "Is *your* maker … alive?"

Joseph looked upward, as if reading the answer in the low ceiling. "Yes. She is."

"Do you have contact with her?"

"Occasionally. Last time was, hmmm … close to 75 years ago I'd guess. I remember traveling to Thebes for her during one of her dark times. She prefers ancient cities to the modern jungle of America."

Thebes. Egypt? Greece? "Dark times?"

He stopped outside the second from last door and pivoted to regard her. A touch of sadness settled into his shifting eyes. "We all have them Dana. That's how I came to meet your Alexander."

Dana waited, a frown crunching her brow.

"I allowed myself to be … captured by a band of vigilantes. Our kind had been outed 15, 20 years before and humans were afraid. Terrified. These men intended to have a morning roast. At the time, I didn't care. I was just so … *tired*. It happens. Your Alex was apparently alerted by all the empty vehicles at the side of the road, not far from a man-made clearing which had likely been … *used* … before." Joseph met her eyes, but they were fathomless. "He pushed me to save myself. Practically dragged me to the cave to dump me inside."

"He never mentioned anything."

"Perhaps he regretted it. I couldn't say. The dark time passed and I dropped by his home to thank him for his assistance." Joseph smiled. "I believe I scared the hell out of him."

"Anyway, it's done." Pushing open the door, he motioned her before him.

It was a small 10x10 windowless room. A single bed jutted from the back wall, bookended by nightstands with single boudoir lamps. Two bookshelves crammed with texts stood directly opposite. "This will be much more comfortable for you. You're welcome to use it as long as you feel necessary."

"Thank you."

"Daylight is almost here." He turned without another word and pulled the door shut behind him.

Wavering less than a moment, she engaged the deadbolt. *Not that it would matter if he really wanted in.*

Unworried, she thought about what he'd said.

Dark times.

All those years spreading before you. How could it not be daunting? As a mortal, you race to finish some nebulous bucket list. What happens when there's no hurry?

Crossing to the bed, Dana lowered herself onto the tapestry spread, mind splitting in several directions at once, confusion muddying the lines between. Images from earlier in the evening seared inside, the psychological merging with the physical distinction of tenderness between her thighs.

God, she had no idea what the hell she was doing anymore.

She'd slept with her best friend ... and managed not to kill him. Despite everything wrong with it, she felt the distinct draw straight back into his arms. If she weakened with another lapse, would he even be so lucky a second time?

No, she wouldn't have another lapse. She couldn't. All those deep, dark bruises shadowed her brain, terrifying her with what could be. What if? Before, Alex had been so strong and solid. Now he seemed weak and fragile.

God. At one time it would never have occurred to her to think of him in those terms, but he was just that.

Vulnerable. Human.

What did it even matter with eternity stretching out before her?

Darkness. Depression. She could easily understand it now.

Shaking her head, she tried to let it go. One thing at a time. A human thought that still made sense. Too much, too soon would overwhelm.

She pondered Joseph opening his home to her and her relenting because she didn't want to sleep amongst garbage. She told herself he was being paternalistic. After all, what decent father wouldn't take steps to protect his children? He'd been horribly burned doing just that. But something in his demeanor bothered her. It was almost like awe, but not quite. She just couldn't quite pinpoint it.

Darkness crackled around the edges to pull her and her brand new tears within. Thoughts bleeding away, Dana curled on her side and was soon lost to the morning sun.

****

Joseph stretched out on his worn sofa, feet crossed on the 1890s steamer trunk he used as a coffee table. Sunlight didn't pull him into an instant black abyss any longer, hadn't for 150 years, give or take. He always enjoyed the quiet at the edge of day and now chose to read a few pages from the 2nd volume of Don Quixote before putting it aside for a chapter of a modern forensic suspense.

The printed page began to blur in the background of an uneasy mind and he soon found himself tossing the paperback next to Cervantes.

He'd brought her into his home and the knowledge warmed but unsettled him. She kept that raw energy of hers muted, but he sensed it was more incidental than purposeful. His instincts hinted that she didn't even recognize the bite of power running just under her flesh.

Yes, definitely unnerving, but it didn't make it any less intriguing.

Through the years he'd only sired a handful of others. They were now scattered all over the planet. At last contact, they'd inhabited New York, Dublin, Taos and Moscow. Each one settled comfortably into the back of his mind, but the connection was always there. If one needed him, he could sense it. Like most grown children, much of the time they didn't.

But none of his other children were like Dana Chambers.

Pushing up, he paced the limited floor space, running a hand through his hair, starting to feel the pull of slumber, but fighting it for a few more moments.

It had to be what she was before. He'd felt it and that, much more than any favor he owed Alex, was the reason he'd changed her. *Something* had made Dana unique against her fellow humans.

The prospect of finding out terrified him, but at the same time, inflated him with exhilaration. Strange quandary to be in, but perhaps, just perhaps, she might be his reason to continue.

Deciding to give in to the day, he walked down the hall, pausing outside Dana's bedroom door. There was a deadbolt affixed inside and he had no doubt she'd engaged it, although truthfully, it was just window dressing. It might deter an average human intruder, but not a healthy vampire.

His pictured her sleeping—rosebud mouth parted just enough to reveal the glint of teeth and soft creamy skin contrasting with the rich chestnut hair spilling over his pillows. A beautiful child.

Stepping away, he shook his head to clear the tangle of thoughts before moving past the door to pursue slumber in the privacy of his own master suite.

Chapter Nineteen

Charles Caras sat at his desk, swiveling his chair to gaze out the large picture window behind him. Slate colored clouds hung low in the sky, heavy and threatening, but rarely allowing more than a steady thirst-quenching rain. Pounding storms that brought the city to a standstill, flooding, and washing away topsoil were uncommon, but he enjoyed the show when the rain came down in opaque sheets turning the world blind.

Pleasure boats of all varieties crisscrossed Lake Washington, owners taking advantage of the weekend, despite the wind stirring and the bitter snap of winter. He vaguely wondered if they'd see snow soon.

His wife kept him abreast of what she and the children were doing on their European jaunt and although he tended to allow her words to merge, he enjoyed the sound of her voice. When she passed the phone to his son, he sat up a little straighter, the phone pressing against his ear a little harder.

At eight, C.J. was wise beyond his years. He caught and analyzed everything and Caras could only imagine how that would benefit him as he matured. Picturing the tow-haired child, he smiled as the boy brought him up to speed regarding their adventures. A moment later, C.J. passed the line to his little sister and her tiny voice pouted at him.

"I miss you, Daddy."

"I miss you, too, sweetie. You'll be home before you know it."

Patricia recovered the phone, wished him love and a good night. Caras disconnected with a tingle of warmth in his chest, which disappeared when he pivoted his chair.

The other presence in the room relaxed in a buttery leather chair across from him, one leg thrown over the opposite knee at the ankle, a clove cigarette pinched between his thumb and forefinger, dark eyes amused as always. "Sounds like the family's having a good time."

Victor took another drag, pushing the acrid smoke from his lungs, waiting with the tiniest of smiles flickering at the corners of thin lips.

Caras hated the smell, but he said nothing.

The situation had become much more complex to the point of insanity. He'd dismissed media reports of vampires with the cavalier attitude of a true skeptic. Now his best man sat before him with information knocking his tidy world askew.

With a deep sigh, he drummed his fingers against the polish of his desk. "You think he can do it?"

The man shrugged with a grin. "Had half his face melted off during one encounter and he climbed back on the horse. Has a pretty tidy record and a team he trusts."

"You'll oversee every move."

"Absolutely. Might even be educational."

Caras absently scratched one eyebrow. To be honest, he wasn't even sure it mattered anymore. How likely would it be that she'd continue her work with the police? He didn't know, he just knew he hated leaving business unfinished. "Okay, Victor. Do it. Only thing I want to hear at this point is your personal verification of a task completed. I don't like loose ends."

"Of course."

"Patricia and the children will be back soon and I just want all this nastiness behind me." He rubbed both hands over his face, suddenly tired. He had too many other concerns and this particular thorn needed to be pulled already.

Victor got to his feet, taking a moment to stub his cigarette out on a mosaic paperweight on the corner of the desk and ignore Caras's glower. "Okay then, boss. I'll give you the heads up when it's all done."

****

Alex followed the waterfront path as it curved past the lake and into the tranquility of the bordering park. Despite the chilly temperatures, residents flocked to the shoreline in droves. Families played in the grass and along the slender patches of sand, teenagers cuddled on benches facing the rich azure of the lake, a mom ran with a jogging stroller, her toddler bundled and screeching with glee, while an old couple walked hand in hand, their mutual breaths mingling as they smiled and chatted.

He'd awakened late morning in denial, sure the night hadn't been any more than an intense dream or, at the very least, an impressively detailed figment of his imagination. But then he'd tried to move.

There was no way to be certain without stepping out into the middle of an intersection in downtown Seattle, but it was very possible getting hit by a bus might be in the same league as making love with a vampire, only without the pleasure principle.

Despite the discomfort of a battered body, Alex held no regrets. Maybe it made him a masochist, but lovesick idiot that he was, he accepted it without complaint. Popping a few ibuprofen before he left the house, he now pushed himself in his run, slowing only when he'd hit his goal.

Dana would, no doubt, feel quite differently about their time together.

Pulling in a full breath, he released it into mist over his lips.

Hazy as it was, he remembered one point in the

night when she thought she may have seriously injured him. Her already fair skin had bleached into bone, dark eyes wide and terrified. He might have even teased her because their easy friendship always merited it, but that was ... before.

Before *everything*.

"Fuck."

A young woman raised an eyebrow when she passed him, a little girl wearing a bright pink coat with pastel bubbles holding tight to her hand.

Alex offered an apologetic smile and the woman easily returned it.

The ticklish feeling of a contemplative gaze on his back followed him. His cop eyes had caught blonde blunt cut hair, light green irises, an eyetooth just barely over one front tooth to create an endearing, if imperfect smile and no wedding ring. The next moment he forgot about her.

Soon he'd have to return to work. Or resign. He wasn't just what his future held any longer. At one time being a cop had been everything to him. Now the importance blurred.

Returning to his truck, he made the familiar trek home, unsure of what came next. Technically, he could extend his leave. He had the time, after all, but he didn't know if that was the right choice either.

He hated the new ambiguity of everything.

Alex pulled the truck into his garage, letting himself into the house through the attached door leading through the kitchen. He headed toward the master bedroom intent on a shower and shave, hoping to feel human again.

The faint aroma of unfamiliar cologne made him pivot a moment before he heard the quiet creak of a floorboard. As instincts and training merged, he sidestepped to the left in time to avoid the blow, whirling to catch the intruder's wrist to give it a hard twist. A grunt of pain reached his ears and the sap thudded against the carpet. Throwing back his head, he connected with his assailant's nose in a crunch of cartilage and bone. A sharp blow from Alex's elbow into a solar plexus drove the breath from the man's lungs and sent him keeling to the floor.

Alex shoved him facedown, planting his knee in the man's back and twisting one burly arm up between his shoulder blades. With the other hand, he reached into his pocket for his cell.

"You fucking broke my nose!" The big man gurgled and spit, anger surpassing injury.

"Shut up." Gritting his teeth, Alex started to hit the number for dispatch when a strong arm snaked around his throat. Dropping the phone, he reached up to lessen the pressure and turn his throat into the crook of the man's elbow. His attacker compensated, pulling him back to press hard against his carotid artery.

Alex tried to jerk to the side to throw his opponent off balance, but weakened when his oxygen starved brain turned his vision gray. A moment later, everything faded into black.

****

Victor held on another moment when Kelly slumped, just to be sure, before rolling him over to bind his wrists

Swearing and glower

ing, Mario kicked the unconscious man in the ribs. "That asshole broke my nose."

"So I saw. You should have been faster." Victor looked at the big man, allowing a trickle of disgust to show. "Now gag him and get him in the truck."

Chapter Twenty

It wasn't quite dark yet, but Mario watched the shadows lengthen as daylight began to ebb, tickling that little center of panic in his brain. Towering firs on either side of the highway seemed to hasten the onset of darkness and a chill pooled between his shoulder blades and into his lower back.

The cabin was still a good twenty miles ahead of them and although Victor remained calm, even cheerful, Mario's gut stayed tight and burning. After all, he'd seen the Chambers woman, his boss hadn't.

Of course, he'd been assured countless times that these other yahoos knew what they were doing, but assurances fell on deaf ears for him. He had seen her both lovely and terrifying. That death mask would haunt him the rest of his life. However long that might be.

"You need to relax." Victor's smooth voice cut into his skittering thoughts. "You're broadcasting your nerves so loudly I can practically hear them twanging."

"Can't help it."

"It's just one woman for God's sake. Yes, I know she's a vampire, but Baker and his guys have put down dozens over the last decade. I'm sure they can handle one little fledgling." Victor pulled his cigarettes from his coat pocket and offered one.

Mario shook his head, figuring he was jumpy enough. The sun would be completely down by five and that didn't give a whole lot of time.

"We don't even know how long it'll take her to find him." Victor lit his own cigarette, gave it a pull and let smoke explode from his lungs. "We might be waiting a while."

"She's fast, man."

"What? She can cover 40 miles in a single bound?"

Feeling the slight sting of foolishness, Mario didn't respond. His nose throbbed like hell and he just wanted to go home, crawl into bed with his voluptuous girlfriend of the month and leave this job in the past. Eyes drifting to the rearview mirror, he jerked his head. "Think he's still out?"

Victor glanced back over his shoulder on impulse, noting the man's still silhouette lying in the bed of the truck. "No. He's back there listening and waiting."

Mario shot him a glance and Victor smiled. "Does it really matter?"

Day continued to ooze from the sky, giving the air a greyish, murky quality. Light overcast clouds would soon bleed into cast iron as the sun dipped beneath the horizon. Mario swallowed, but bit back a huge sigh a moment later when he caught sight of his turnoff.

"Not too much further." Victor raised his brows with a smirk. "Where's your sense of adventure?"

"I like my adventure on the big screen. Don't need to live it." Mario kept his eyes on the road, trying without success to whitewash all the niggling fears.

"You sadden me, my friend."

Mario left the highway and took the truck onto a narrow two-lane road with asphalt crumbling at the edges and potholes dimpling the rest. Trees pressed in to form a tunnel above and he flipped the headlights on, stomach tightening into a painful boulder. The cabin was isolated, better for disposal, but also further away from help if things went wrong.

His boss would say he was having a glass-half-empty kind of day. Victor enjoyed being flippant to a fault and Mario accepted it, knowing that seemingly carefree attitude hid an individual who lived and killed by his own warped sense of ethics. He could be one scary son of a bitch, but at the moment, Mario couldn't decide whether it was his boss or the vampire woman who scared him more.

To save himself some embarrassment, he figured he'd just take a piss the second they arrived. Just to be on the safe side.

****

Victor tilted his head and examined the ancient A-frame cabin. It was shabby, with a half dozen missing shingles and cracked glass in one front window. Faded paint that may have resembled hunter green in another lifetime clung to its exterior in peeling flaps. After changing hands dozens of times over the years, it now was a cancerous blemish for the forestry service.

Ugly as it was, structurally speaking, it was sound. It stood miles from its closest neighbor and inhabited enough of a clearing to accommodate a small barbeque without the worry of taking half the forest with it.

Two pickups and a foreign all-wheel drive sedan flowered out from the five steps leading up to a sagging front deck. Between all three vehicles, he saw enough bumper sticker rhetoric to bring a sour taste to the back of his tongue and a bitterness to his spirit. He shook it off and considered the source. "Looks like the party started without us."

Mario grunted, gravel crunching beneath the tires as he pulled behind the sedan and cut the engine.

A moment later, Baker appeared just outside the tattered screen door, his damaged face pale in the waning light, rifle slung over his back in a deceptively casual stance. The man's sharp eyes roamed, alert and ready. He nodded at Victor, but didn't approach.

"Okay, then. Let's go ahead and make our guest comfortable." He climbed from Kelly's truck, letting the door slam and startling several birds from the treetops.

Mario's breath whistled through his damaged nose as he followed and Victor made a mental note to keep a close watch. He didn't want the man's temper to pop off and dispatch Kelly prematurely. A dead man would be useless as bait.

He opened the tailgate and hatch of the truck's canopy to find the cop curled on his side, eyes open, clear, and seething. Blood leaked from his wrists where he'd fought with his bindings.

Without a word, Mario stepped up at the same moment Kelly twisted to plant both running shoe clad feet in the huge man's groin. All color bleached from his face and he dropped to his knees, holding his crotch. Loud wheezing sounds emanated from him while he tried to recover his breathing.

"None of that." Hiding his surprise, Victor yanked his 9 mm from his shoulder harness and pressed it under Kelly's chin. "Keep in mind, I'm not going to kill you right now no matter what foolishness you pull, but I *can* make your time here *very* uncomfortable."

Holding the gun steady, Victor grabbed Kelly's arm to pull him from the vehicle, before giving him a searching look. With one quick motion, he yanked the patch of duct tape from the man's mouth and Kelly winced. "I don't think you'll need that up here. Might even be to our advantage if you make a little noise. I'm really not sure how this whole vampire lover thing works."

Alex set his jaw, saying nothing.

"Son of a bitch." His complexion holding a greenish hue, Mario staggered to his feet, shooting a death look at the cop. Without hesitation, he buried his fist in the man's midsection.

All air shoved out in a sudden whoosh, Alex crumpled forward. Gravel and grit bit into the side of his face when momentum brought him folding to the ground, gasping.

Victor smirked and shook his head. "Get Mr. Kelly to his feet, please."

Growling like a wounded bear, Mario roughly pulled the man upright and dragged him up the wooden steps and through the front door.

Chapter Twenty-One

Dana went on alert the moment the sun dropped beyond the Pacific. Despite total darkness, her eyes slashed through the room, seeing what would have been impossible at one time. The room was uncluttered, but comfortable. Her memory clicked. She was in Joseph's home.

The now familiar hunger wove around her insides, pulsating and painful, alive in its insistence. Sitting up, she wrapped her arms around her midsection, wincing at the turmoil inside, half expected an alien to burst from her and run for it.

Intent on feeding, she gritted her teeth and made her way from the small bedroom, through the underground living area and upstairs into the sterile façade her maker hid behind.

"If you plan on going to Maggie's, you're more than welcome to ride with me." Joseph stood at the front picture window, staring into the blackness of his property, his hands shoved into his pockets. When he turned, his corneas were as dark as the view behind him, skin light grey and haggard.

A pang of sadness bounced around beyond the hunger, knowing she resembled a monster as much as Joseph did. Maybe even more. She wondered how Alex would react if he saw her like this.

The emotional blow came from nowhere and she reeled forward. Reaching out, she caught hold of the back of the sofa to keep from sinking to the floor. Pain reverberated in her mind and she squeezed her eyes closed to stem it.

"Dana? What is it?"

Some small part was aware of Joseph's hand on her, the rest breaking into sharp, jagged pieces as emotional and physical distress washed over and through her. Despite the emptiness of her system, violent sickness rose up her throat, tearing and searing and making her gag. "Something's wrong."

Joseph's brows drew together in a heavy frown. "What are you talking about?"

"I have to go." Drawing herself up, she pushed aside the ravages of her body's demands and darted for the door.

He caught her before she could escape, fingers gripping her bicep, firm, but not painful. "I don't understand what's going on, but if you don't feed, you'll compromise yourself."

"Let go." She snapped the words out from between bared teeth. "Now."

Opening his mouth to argue, he shut it just as quickly as the low hum vibrated through him, making his insides tremble and his skin creep with the sensation of thousands of marching insects. Just beyond him, the windows shuddered and wood beams groaned.

Her expression hardened, emotions whipping through her in waves, pounding over him, threatening to drive him to the floor. Releasing her, he backed away, fear, confusion, and beyond that, amazement and intrigue soaked into him.

Snarling, her gaunt face pulled into a death mask, while her bleeding dark eyes guaranteed to drive the bravest of humans away. Without another word or warning, she dissolved into the blackness, the front door gaping behind her.

Joseph watched her become a pinpoint in the distance, knowing she was going to Alexander, wondering if the tie should to be broken before it was too late.

****

A cheery fire cracked and popped to diminish the evening chill as darkness folded across the cabin. Electric lights from an ancient generator staved off the shadows, but did nothing to dispel the underlying tension within the old building.

"Fucker." Mario stood near, eyeing the cop, while Alex tried not to retch in the corner of the mildew stained couch where he'd just been dumped. The big guy believed in retribution and he'd landed on the receiving end of several brutal kicks to the stomach and groin. He was pretty certain his balls tried to crawl up into his belly in a valiant attempt to save themselves.

Despite waves of pain, nausea, and dizziness, he kept his eyes open, studying his surroundings, scrutinizing each man. The four new faces in the old building pretended to be at ease, cracking jokes, laughing with bravado that didn't put a dent in the thickness of the atmosphere. Alex mentally dubbed them Scarface, Ponytail, Flannel, and Kid. The last, barely twenty, pushed aside the ragged curtain to peek out the front window and the reflection glinting back lost good humor in the private moment.

Feigning borderline consciousness, he shifted his observation to the big man, smelling his fear like body odor. Beyond the anger, Mario's skin stretched pale over a wide sweat streaked face. Terror settled into the worried grooves of his flesh, transforming the rough features into that of an oversized frightened child.

Interesting. He knew something his boss didn't.

Alex watched and waited until Victor cruised away to speak to the tall, gangly man with horrific scars and a rifle slung over his shoulder. As he observed, he brought it around, sliding the bolt, showing off the simple elegance of the weapon, the ruined face crinkling in a smile. Narrowing his gaze, it occurred to him something about the weapon was off, but his muddled mind couldn't identify what the difference might be. Shaking his head, he stopped when the cabin tilted around him.

****

Glancing over, Victor eyed Kelly, impressed with the man's blank countenance. Beneath that detached look, he knew his thoughts were moving in rapid succession. Bound hands or not, if he did slide past them, what would his plan be? Get out the door and into the relative shelter of the woods? Not likely. Kelly was too smart. He knew he'd just earn himself a bullet in the knee.

No, Victor didn't worry about the cop. Dana Chambers, however, did concern him. Not that it would ever reflect beyond the internal. His discomfort mostly took the shape of the unexpected. He hated knowing the framework but not the meat of the plan. Baker was a tight-lipped son-of-a-bitch, choosing the ambiguous road of case by case. His crew appeared relaxed around a core of steel. With the exception of the kid, they all were hardened by years of outdoor work, with leathery skin, John Deere caps, and tattoos melted into blotches. Tough, capable men. Victor had only been advised to keep himself and his man clear.

Although it might prove to be a very interesting evening, he held a security blanket in the form of his favorite handgun. He kept the Browning clean, oiled and ready. It was difficult to imagine any creature that couldn't be felled by segmented hollow points, vampires included. All the folklore was ridiculous. If he turned out to be wrong, at the very least he had Kelly. Personal attachments could be such a bitch. That's why Victor avoided them.

"Probably won't be too long. Newbies cling to their old lives and if this guy is as important to it as you think," Baker jerked his head toward the man slumped on the couch. "It'll make a beeline here. Just be ready and don't ever underestimate."

The kid swallowed. "It's just a girl, right?"

"Uh huh. And a Great White is just a fish. Fledglings aren't *usually* much of a problem, but you still can't take 'em for granted. You can never forget what you're dealin' with." Baker stared at Victor, one eye sagging. "You might want to get comfy with your cop friend. Worst case scenario happens and he might be the difference between us all walking away to live and fuck another day or getting ripped apart like sheep."

Face colorless, the kid cradled his rifle to him like a teddy bear, eyes darting like a rabbit's. Ponytail patted him on the shoulder, offering a low word of comfort.

Victor stared back at Baker, galled. He wasn't one to take orders from inferiors, but he accepted he was out of his element. With effort, he swallowed the acidic comment lurking at the tip of his tongue.

****

Dana made her way northeast, the cold wind slapping her face and hair, her muscles flexing and moving with fluid ease. If circumstances were different, if she didn't feel sick and agitated, she might have even enjoyed herself. A distant part of her still marveled at her speed and ability to leap, having first likened her motion to that of a vampiric flea. The flip thought didn't even come close to her consciousness now—tension, rage, and terror curling into a poisonous serpentine cocktail.

Alex's aura led her, but the intense emotions running through him seeped deep within, thrashing around, threatening to cripple her if she didn't manage them.

She was close now.

Trees twisted around her, sheltering, comforting. She'd always been at ease with the rugged landscape of the Pacific Northwest. As a child, she saw beauty where some saw bleak isolation.

Stopping, her gaze cut through the night, lured by dim lights.

The ancient cabin stood in a clearing some 300 yards away and she settled back to observe. Seven inside. Alex's aura was bookended by two others that had her leaning forward onto her knees and stifling a gag. She knew them. One had followed her from her home to Maggie's and the other had stood outside her home *that* night. They converged, oily and cloying, blocking her senses, marring her concentration.

No. She couldn't allow it. She couldn't let the darkness impede her.

Alex was too close to the others. Energy reserves tapped and hunger torturous, she didn't know how fast she could get in and out, without risking his safety.

How invulnerable was she? It hadn't been something she'd discussed with Joseph. He'd warned her of daylight but nothing else. She didn't feel invincible with the hunger raging and her head pounding though. She felt like a sick … human.

Part of her discomfort stemmed from her connection with Alex. He'd been hurt, battered, and those effects ran through her own body as second nature. The knowledge burned her temper even brighter.

A shadow moved past the window to the far left and she smiled, a low rumbling growl generating just below her diaphragm.

Chapter Twenty-Two

They spoke of her as a *thing*, an animal with no value if not for the sport of eradication.

Mario shoved him aside to drop next to him and Alex bared his teeth. Rage trembled within his muscles and blood. He'd become the proverbial worm on the hook, just an emotional lure to bring Dana out of hiding.

And he knew she would come. At least as long as she could sense his aura.

The front door stood less than twenty feet away, but if he even made a run for it, they wouldn't kill him, at least not yet, but he would wind up with a bullet in his leg for his trouble.

No, they wouldn't kill him *on purpose*, but perhaps they'd do it by accident or temper.

It would break the chain. Dana would have no reason to come here at that point. No life, no aura, no Dana.

The knot inside pulling tight, he studied Mario.

The big man's face scrunched together, tension and panic rippling his face, even as he tried desperately to hide it. He looked beyond him and stared out into the night, eyes flickering back and forth, his fingers white against the butt of his Glock.

"Scared, Mario?" Alex looked to the blatant fear as an opening. Tilting his head, he tunneled his gaze on the other man. "You ever see what a vampire can do to a human?"

"Shut up."

"It's not pretty. Did you know they can rip your head right from your body?"

"I said shut up." The man licked his lips, sweat

gleaming on his cheeks, fists bunching. Standing just to the side of the first window, the scarred man turned to cast a glance their way and borderline amusement rippled over what was left of his face. Ponytail stood next to him and smirked.

Alex ignored them, concentrating on the man who wore his fear so brightly. "I heard about an incident where one vamp slaughtered six armed men. They're so fucking fast. But you know that, don't you Mario?"

Victor dropped down just to his left, hand hovering near his weapon, eyes moving in a continuous arc, ugly-handsome face rigid, but he looked toward Alex and raised a brow.

"I wouldn't goad him if I were—" Victor cut off the advice and sighed.

The vicious blow snapped Alex's head back and lights sparkled and dimmed behind his eyes.

"As I was saying, I wouldn't goad him if I were you. He's got a bit of a short—"

The window furthest from the door imploded in a shower of jagged shards, a shrill, otherworldly scream reverberating within the confines of the small cabin.

Alex lifted his ringing head just in time to see a ravaged white face appear for less than a second before Ponytail was wrenched through to disappear into the night. His scream rose and fell, echoing among the trees as Scarface leveled his rifle, with unruffled calm. The report of two shots sliced the stillness before he pulled back inside and away from the window.

"Oh, my God. Oh, my God. Oh, fuck. Oh, Jesus." Body frozen, eyes bulging, the boy chanted for several seconds until Flannel smacked him on the side of the head.

In the distance, Ponytail screamed again, but the cry cut off and the forest stilled.

A low moaning sound filled the space next to him as Mario's breath rose and fell in trembling gusts. His hand gripped Alex's bicep, threatening to cut off circulation and bringing out a wince.

Any forming plan stuck in the back of his brain as he tried to make sense of what he just witnessed. In that fleeting moment, he captured a glimpse of something completely unrecognizable. Death white, cavernous eyes, sharp cutting bones. Something of nightmares. Sickness welled inside, but he steeled himself and choked it down.

It wasn't unprecedented. He'd seen a hungry vampire before.

Dana was no different.

Face grim, Scarface sighed and braced his rifle up against his shoulder. "Well, that sucked, but there *is* good news."

For the first time, Victor looked shaken. "What possible good news could you *have*? I could be mistaken, but one of your men was just … yanked screaming out the window."

The man smiled and shook his head. "The good news *is* I'm fairly sure I shot your target."

****

Dana fed from the man, somehow summoning the strength to stop before she killed him. Alcohol and tobacco lessened the flavor, but new strength flowed through her when the hunger eased.

Dropping him, she ignored the soft grunt and watched the cabin. The chorus of shocked screams had faded and the quiet of frightened expectation seeped into the perimeter.

At full strength, she knew she could slide in and out and they wouldn't know what happened. The urge to kill them all throbbed inside like something rotten, but she couldn't allow it.

An insect itched the back of her shoulder and she took a swipe, eyes still fastened to the cabin. Her movement knocked something into the undergrowth and she paused, reaching to pick it up between her forefinger and thumb.

A chill coursed through her veins.

She'd been darted like some kind of rogue animal.

Curling lips from her fangs, the deep growl vibrated through her body. Anger reddened her vision and she headed back to the cabin, determined to pull Alex out, but now uncertain about the survival of the others.

****

Sociopaths must have been on clearance at the local parole office.

Hazy and ridiculous thoughts entered Alex's mind as he looked around the small cabin. Between Victor, Mario and Scarface, he'd had his quota filled for the evening. The surreal quality of the night made him wonder if his sanity was thumbing its nose at him.

A low hum filled the air and that intense vibration pushed through to rattle his teeth and cut through his insides. *Nope. His sanity hadn't departed.* The moment of relief was fleeting. He remembered the surge of power stroking over him that night Dana first appeared to him and she hadn't even been aware of it. Her gift had somehow evolved and he had no clue what it had evolved *into*. Gritting his teeth, he could only wait and watch helplessly. Sliding to the floor seemed a sound choice, but the big man held onto him with iron manacles.

****

"What the hell is *that*?" The boy's tone spiked into a pitch rivaling a castrato.

It rose in frequency as heavy waves hit, rattling doors, glass and the entire framework of the cabin.

Uneasy, Victor shot a fast glance toward Baker, seeing confusion and fear blaring across the scarred features. The man's eyes rounded and rolled like a panicking horse.

This couldn't be normal.

A dark foreboding shimmered inside his belly. For the first time ever, his instincts told him to run, but pride made him hesitate. He'd never been a coward.

The thick vibration rose up and over them, suffocating, unrelenting. Tendrils of snakes began to twist and writhe inside his head and he pressed the heel of his hand above his eyes.

If you don't run, you're going to die. A harsh voice whispered up at him from deep in his soul. *Fuck saving face.*

Mario gaped at him when he rose. "Victor?"

There was a backdoor off the kitchen. He passed Baker, who frowned and reached out a long-fingered hand to catch his forearm. "Weird time to take a piss."

Shaking the man off, he ignored the raised voices following him.

A step from escape, the front door burst open. He shot a look over his shoulder just as he pushed through the flimsy back exit and didn't look again. On legs willing to betray him, he took advantage of Dana Chambers's distraction and dove into the night.

****

Despite the yawning and creaking sounds of strained lumber, Dana's entrance was silent, movements feline and graceful, dark eyes soaking in the situation. She met Alex's stare and his heart rabbited when heavy emotions tangled into a mess of unresolved issues to line his stomach with acid. She was so lovely, skin creamy porcelain with a touch of pink in her cheeks indicating her recent feeding, but fury had settled into her features instead of hunger, making her no less terrifying.

She narrowed in on Mario's weapon and the vibration intensified, becoming painful. Her lips pulled back from her teeth, a low growl filling the room, but she didn't move forward.

"Oh, shit. Oh, fuck. Oh, shit. Oh, fuck." The boy stepped back, chanting oath after oath, not even trying to disguise his terror.

"Shouldn't be much longer." Scarface held his rifle ready, worry replacing his earlier arrogance. He seemed to weigh the possibility of using his weapon again against the time it would take her to rip him to pieces. "Shut up, Evan. You're giving me a headache."

The boy continued on in a hoarse whisper.

"You need to get the hell away from him." She didn't have to raise her voice, the growl bouncing off the interior of the cabin.

Mario stared at her before his shocked gaze dropped to the weapon he pointed at Kelly. A moment later, his face hardened. "I know you're fast. I've seen it, but if you kill me, my finger could jerk and spray his brains all over this ugly old couch."

Alex clenched his jaw, concentrating on her face, hearing a low hiss somewhere deep inside his head, but rising with the edge of a hurricane.

She blinked once, slowly and his stomach curdled. Scarface said he'd shot the target. Realization hit him and Alex pulled in a sharp breath. The man hadn't been using bullets. That's what had been bugging him earlier. He'd used a tranquilizer dart.

"I think you're all going to die," Alex whispered.

Chapter Twenty-Three

Dana's anger surged outward. All those vile auras, housed in and around decayed and twisted individuals. They'd been there, haunting her, the moment she'd opened her eyes after the accident and over the last couple of years, draining her, slowly killing her. She remembered her neurologist warning of possible side effects down the line. Of course, they'd just been guesses, considering she was his pet lab monkey. But he'd been right. Even when she didn't want to analyze it, her subconscious was there, whispering of bad omens, pain, and death.

The air boiled around her, confusing her, but the vicious movement of the storm felt as natural as breathing once had. Energy flowed across them in response to Dana's anger and pain. It crackled, searing and uncomfortable.

"Whatever you're doing, you need to stop!" Mario barked, fear quivering in his voice.

"I don't think she can help it." Whatever was happening was beyond her control. Alex could see the strain and fear as she fought her rage.

"Don't worry. That tranq could drop a fucking elephant. Whatever the hell this is, it should be over soon." Scarface frowned, terror and confusion pressing into the distorted features, his voice shaking.

Mario parted his lips to respond, but in the same moment his gun hand began to shake and he opened his mouth in a silent scream instead. Alex took advantage and threw himself forward, landing hard on the scuffed floor. Twisting his wrists, he tried to free himself from the plastic binding, but his gaze remained locked in horrified fascination. Even as he watched, pain began to twist and turn within his own head and an itching of fear made him wonder if his own fate would match the men around him.

Waves undulated just below Mario's skin and his body convulsed, screams gaining a voice now, insistent and full of agony. Something alive seemed determined to burst from him.

What the hell was this?

The auras were no longer indicators of a person's ethics. They'd become something larger than her, larger than anyone.

****

Body trembling, power roared through her body and she couldn't do a damn thing about it, nor did she want to. Her anger had shifted into something alive and the only thing she could do was try to keep it from touching Alex.

Opening up, she concentrated to allow their vile auras to invade and pulverize the rest of them from the inside out, now knowing she didn't even have to touch them to make them bleed.

The hemorrhaging began at their eyes and at one time she would have been horrified, but all the fury inside did not quell. It flowed through her, bringing such intensity her insides vibrated with it. The scarred man danced in a macabre puppet show, losing his sight in a spray of blood and eye jelly, while the others dropped as fluid gushed from all other orifices. The boy took several wobbly steps toward the door before going still, as if frozen in terror. Less than a minute later, he dropped into a puddle of his own life's liquid. *Oh, God, he was just a boy!* She ignored the human wail inside her head as the screams became gurgles and bodies thumped to the floor, twitching. The man who'd held Alex at gunpoint had gaping holes where his eyes had been, face covered in gore. She watched his fingers curl when the last breath left him. His aura drifted from him and evaporated.

Her eyes swept the interior. One was missing. Darkly, she considered she'd get him later.

The sudden quiet shocked as much as the demolished bodies at her feet. She continued to tremble, even as the power ebbed and her mind dulled.

Her body weakened from exertion, drugs, or both, pushed the hunger to rear its head. It was a natural response—energy out needed energy in. There was blood everywhere, but she couldn't feed from corpses. Vampires weren't scavengers. The very prospect disgusted her and her stomach lurched in response.

Keeping her movements slight, she pivoted her head toward Alex. He lay on the filthy floor, hands bound behind him. Thin trickles of blood ran from his left nostril and right ear. The anguish tore her insides into pieces. She'd tried to protect him but apparently it wasn't enough. *My dear Alex* ... emotions swirled around her, digging in. She loved him. No more confusion.

Dana walked toward him, dropping into a crouch and snapping his bindings with ease before scrambling away. She shouldn't be near him. She was too dangerous now. A wave of despair brought pain deep into her belly.

"I... I'm so sorry..." The words sounded so inconsequential, meaningless. She'd been turned into a vampire, yes, but she'd also been turned into something else. Something indefinable.

He pushed to his feet, brilliant eyes fixed on her face.

"Don't." She shook her head and waved him away, but couldn't put a lot of power behind it. Her muscles liquefied from beneath her, strength gone.

Alex didn't let her fall. He never did. Bundling

her against his solid frame, he slid strong arms under her knees and behind her shoulders.

The hunger spiked and she closed her eyes, trying to concentrate, trying to sequester it into a tiny little box deep inside, but it wouldn't be contained. So much energy had been expelled and her body insisted on replenishment. She could already picture her black corneas. How alien and horrific they must be to him.

"I think I know what you need right now." He murmured, like he was comforting a child. It was the same tone she used to use when she babysat her nephews and the youngest was frightened by a trick of moonlight and shadows merging into a monster. At the time she'd told him monsters weren't real.

Moisture cooled on her face and she brought one trembling hand up to skirt fingertips under her eyes, certain it would come away slick with sprayed blood from one of these men she'd murdered. Marginally surprised, she found the liquid clear. She hadn't been aware of her tears.

"Dana." Alex brushed his lips against her temple.

She settled her arms around him, pushing her face against his heat, artery throbbing under her lips. He pressed a kiss to the top of her head, another tiny nod to the depth of his feelings as they lay surrounded by horror.

"I'm so sorry…"

"It's okay, honey. You're okay." His whisper quivered with pain and she winced.

She didn't think the situation was okay by any stretch and she knew he didn't either, but his gentle voice reminded her he would do anything and everything within his power to make it so.

It was true. She should stay away, but as she gazed at him, she knew it would be impossible. Blinking slowly, she could feel the drug beckoning. It remained persistent in its job to send her into premature oblivion, just as her hunger split through her, cruel and unwavering. Her body seemed determined to rip itself in two. "I used you."

He frowned at her, tilting his head. "I don't think so."

Ignoring his response, she whispered against his skin. "I did. I don't think I can ever be ... me, again."

Control became a quality tumbling in the dust, gasping its final breaths behind her. The shame overwhelmed, but the primal need was more so. She sank her fangs into his throat and drank deep. He pulled in a sudden breath, but didn't jerk away. She could have sworn his arms tightened in response and the thought didn't surprise her.

His blood flowed through her, sweet, savory and spicy, everything she needed and wanted in that moment. It was serotonin tickling her brain, bringing her close to ecstasy, orgasmic in its intensity. A vivid memory invaded her head, one of writhing beneath and above him in sweaty, primal passion and her loins tightened in response. The blood heated her belly and spiraled through the rest of her body, looking to capture lost strength, fighting whatever powerful narcotic her would-be assassins had pumped into her.

****

Dana drank in more and they slid to the floor together. He feared he'd lose any remaining strength when her fangs left his throat as smoothly as they'd entered. Alex looked down to see her eyes glassy but clearing. Blood dribbled over her lips. *His blood.*

Cradling her to him, he couldn't move, muscles betraying, body shaking when shadows stirred before his eyes. He blinked with force to push them away, trying to tune his fuzzy brain. Gently, he pushed her hair back from her face. "You okay?"

She frowned up at him. "I think so.

Do not pass out, God damn it! He smiled, despite the struggle inside. "So much for dropping a small elephant."

Dana blinked and sat up. "Feel a little dopey, but it seems to be burning off. We need to get going."

Beyond the pounding in his head, he watched, transfixed, as she morphed into complete health. Her eyes transitioned back to their lovely tawny with darker brown flecks, her skin glowing, color returning to her cheeks. It took him a long moment to register what she'd said. "Get going?"

Something flickered in her beautiful eyes, and a chill ran through him. There was nothing benign about it. "The one who ran, Alex. I need to find him."

Alex wrapped his muddled mind around her words. The smaller, dark-haired man. The one who'd been holding the big guy's leash. Not the top man, but judging from his demeanor, close to him. If he led them to his employer, they might be able to end this.

But Jesus, more death, more darkness. He'd been catapulted down this dire path and he had no idea how to stop it. Physically, he could walk away. Emotionally and psychologically, it wasn't going to happen. He'd stay by her side, wherever it led them. The life he knew, however long it might last, was now gone.

Dana crouched near, staring at him, unblinking. "You should go home, Alex."

****

He clenched his teeth, wincing. "Aspirin would be good, but I'll deal."

Tilting her head, she regarded him. He was battered and much too pale, but a familiar and determined light brightened his eyes. He wanted to help end this, but he'd almost been killed tonight. She couldn't leave him here, but she wanted him safe.

He pushed himself toward Mario's body, careful to avoid as much gore as possible and leaned over to search through his pockets. "Keys to my truck, because I can't move like you can."

Pulling the ring from the dead man's overcoat, he stared down at them before looking up at Dana, face waxy. "Hell, I'm not sure I can move at all right now."

Within a blink, she hauled him to his feet, one arm snug around his waist, while his draped over her shoulders. Alex almost commented about how ludicrous they must look, but the words didn't quite make it out.

****

When Dana wrangled him into his truck, he was unresponsive, head lolling against his chest. Sickness cramped her belly. He was alive, she could smell it, but she delicately touched the side of his neck out of habit, relieved to find his pulse strong.

Frowning, she brushed at the clotted blood clinging to his throat. She'd just fed, but the skin was unbroken, marks already healed into small scars. Had he healed faster than before? Was that possible?

Shaking her head to clear any residual drug from her mind, she double checked his belt restraints were secure before crawling into the driver's seat. The night was nowhere near over.

Chapter Twenty-Four

Victor tried to keep the rasping of his breath in check. Sweat coated his face and he swiped an arm over it with the sleeve of his $2,000 coat, quickly returning his hand to the steering wheel. The little sports wagon he'd boosted from the cabin was so far out of alignment he needed the extra muscle to keep it centered in his lane. Any wavering would attract police attention and that was the last thing he needed.

He'd always prided himself on not getting rattled, but baser instincts flared up to tangle with his practiced calm. Victor could only tamp it down to avoid doing anything reckless. He needed to remain logical.

The woman hadn't seen him. At least he didn't think so. She'd also been tranquilized and, according to Baker, it would put her down the rest of the night. Did he say would or *should*? Or did he even say at all? Victor couldn't quite remember.

No, no, that had to have been it. Tranq them and lay them out for the sun to dispose of. Baker had been doing it for years, with only one mishap and that had involved kerosene and a lighter. He'd said he'd found the sun to be the only foolproof method.

Well, technically, two mishaps, and Victor doubted the man had survived this second one. The chorus of painful, anguished screams rang in his ears when he'd been fumbling under the seat for hidden car keys. A shudder ran though his muscles at the memory and he gripped the wheel tighter.

In theory, Dana Chambers shouldn't be tracking him. She should now be in the vampire equivalent of a coma. He could go home, check in with Caras, and determine his next move. If he deemed it necessary, he could be on a plane before the night's end.

Of course, that was a lot of supposition. Victor didn't know a lot about vampires, but he was fairly certain those intense waves of power he'd experienced weren't the norm. It had felt heavy, electric, pulsing into and through him, bringing a sting to his flesh and a thickness to his brain.

Victor had always been dubious regarding psychics and paranormal bullshit, but Chambers had definitely had a talent for tracking people. Whatever that talent had been as a human had evolved into something else as a vampire.

Taking a chance by removing one hand from the wheel, he yanked his cell from his coat pocket to call Caras, sandwiching it between his ear and shoulder.

The man picked up at the second ring. "Is it done?"

Victor pulled in a long breath. "There's a problem."

He heard the crinkle of movement and waited, trying to form a response for something he couldn't explain.

"What kind of problem?"

"It would seem she is not a normal vampire."

The secured line slid into silence and Victor held onto the car's wheel, watching freeway exits, wondering if he shouldn't bother and just continue south to the airport. There were many possible destinations dancing in his head. All of them warm.

"What exactly does that mean?"

"I'm not even sure. Baker darted her when she grabbed one of his men. After that, all hell broke loose. Everyone's dead." He hadn't stayed around long enough to find out for sure, but his gut insisted it to be true.

"Everyone, except you."

The man's tone aggravated already raw nerves and Victor curved a lip. "Yes. If you'd been there, you'd also be dead. Your order to have this woman terminated has just blown up in your fucking face. If I were you, I'd start watching my back."

"Is that a threat, Victor?" Caras growled and Victor smiled, making his decision. He'd be flying to South America before the sun came up.

"No, but I'd take it as a warning. Whatever allowed this woman to track and take down your men has turned into something nastier than just a vampire. The power rushing through her is something I've never experienced and you know, I've experienced *a lot* in my professional life." Victor glanced down to the dash when the low gas warning light came on and frowned.

Caras said nothing, but Victor could hear the rushing of agitated breaths. "What are our options?"

Run. Run as fast as you can. "Tip the media. This woman is not only dangerous to humans, but, I think, to her own kind as well. Other vamps might elect to take her out. Wash your hands of the problem."

"All right. Stay the hell away from me, but don't leave the city. I'll be in touch." Caras disconnected without waiting for an answer.

"Yeah, sure, boss." Disbelieving, Victor bared his teeth, anger at his employer rubbing intimately against his fear of Chambers. Fuck the Greek. He had every intention of falling off the radar. Seattle would soon be a bad memory.

He guided the car off the freeway, intent on his future, already visualizing it. He had multiple accounts off American soil, so retiring young was an easy option. Of course, if boredom dictated, he wasn't averse to picking up jobs here and there. His skills were highly sought among a certain cliental.

Pulling up to the outermost pump, he jogged into the convenience store to pay cash and grab some crappy coffee. He returned to the little car, stopping abruptly and staring. His bladder loosened and only through sheer will did he not urinate on himself.

Dana Chambers leaned against the driver's side, hands shoved in the slash pockets of her coat. She smiled at him. "Hi, there."

The woman's complexion was cream with soft rose touching her cheeks. Glossy hair tumbled past her shoulders, disheveled in a sexy bedroom way, triggering flutters of fantasy deep within his lizard brain. Dark eyes, the color of expensive bourbon, met his and ice shards slicing through his belly began to melt and warm. A haze filled his brain as he gazed at her. The distant echo of panic faded away and he smiled back.

"What's your name?" Her voice carried a smoky quality fused with silk.

"Victor Alvarez."

She straightened and stepped closer to him. "Well, Mr. Alvarez, you and I have something to discuss. I think a little drive might be in order. What do you think?"

"Whatever you'd like."
****

Dale Pritchett army crawled because he couldn't do much else. That thing had grabbed him, bitten him and dumped him in a pile of pine needles, dead branches, and exposed roots. His head still spun and wove, even as he tried to still it.

The screaming had stopped and as far as he could tell, his hadn't been involved in that ghastly chorus echoing from the cabin, through the trees, and seemingly bouncing off the very sky itself. It did still ebb and surge in his brain and he wished he had the strength to shut it off. Dale thought he may have blacked out once or twice and some part of him wished he would again. The other part wanted to kick his ass for even thinking that.

Pushing his body forward, he grabbed handfuls of foliage and sharp stones, wondering if he'd grabbed onto poison oak. Wait, would that even be around during winter? He couldn't focus, but figured poisonous plants were likely the least of his problems. Just at the edge of the clearing, he blinked dull eyes toward the front of the cabin, noting the jagged window where he'd been pulled through.

But he was alive. Murky as his brain was, the single thought remained crystalline even if wrapped in confusion. When the pale-faced she-devil grabbed onto him with steel talons, he should have been dead. For a moment, he thought he was, when the demon disappeared and the beautiful angel took its place. It had been a fleeting moment when he hung between life and death and he'd memorized what he saw, maybe to tell his family when he came back from hell.

Now he knew he hadn't died. The cold impaled him from one end to the other and his body ached from dozens of bruises and cuts. He knew now that the creature had just changed its appearance after feeding from him.

Worry about hypothermia glazed over him as his body shook and his hands and toes numbed. He pushed to his feet, fell onto the gravel with a strangled oath and tried again. His legs refused to hold his weight, but he made them with a determination and tenacity his mother would be proud of.

Dale didn't want to go into the cabin, but his curiosity outweighed his common sense as he passed by his truck to place one foot on the lowest sagging step leading to the porch. He stared up beyond the broken door, making a valiant effort to stop himself, but unable to do it. He had to see, had to *know*.

The smell hit him first, the foul odor of excrement mingling with blood and bile. Clenching his jaw, he created a mental mantra to keep from vomiting and stepped inside. His face sagged and a wave of faintness washed over him. He shoved it back, moving forward, keeping the presence of mind to watch where he placed his feet.

God, God, God. They were all dead, eyes gone, rivulets of blood coagulating from ears, noses. Baker's nails had popped along with his fingertips and the bones stuck out, a glint of white in a wash of gore. What the fuck was this? No vampire could do something like this. A quick meal of pastrami and cheese on wheat from earlier in the evening rose in his throat, burning, seeking escape.

Slow realization seeped in from what his eyes gazed upon.

They'd want to cover this up. Hide this horror. If *he* were responsible, he'd want to destroy everything, which meant, they'd be back.

Dale twisted around, tangled in his feet and landed in the gelatinous pool that had oozed from the big guy. For a long moment his mouth worked and no sound came out. The long scream finally broke through and he cut it off with one hand, the sound muted, vibrating, but threatened to overwhelm him until he wouldn't be able to stop.

Must leave now.

He managed to get some traction underneath him and pushed toward the door, half crawling out into the cold night. With the hunger of someone oxygen deprived, he gulped the mountain air into his lungs, but the smell of death lingered in his sinuses, the taste on his tongue. Twisting, he stumbled toward his truck and ran right into the newcomer.

Falling backward, Dale pinwheeled his arms to keep balance, failed and landed on his ass with a yelp.

****

Joseph stared at the human at his feet, taking in the pale flesh and bloodied neck. He cocked his head to the side, considering. Dana had fed from this one, but left him alive. That had probably been intentional on her part. The horror he smelled inside, however, had not been. She'd lost control. Whatever that wonderful power was, the men inside had experienced it firsthand. He was a little sorry he'd stayed away. He'd felt the transition of her worry into fury, but had resisted going to her. A tiny part of him feared her, but he tucked the admission away, more comfortable with the likelihood she hadn't needed him.

He dropped into a crouch before the man, who stared unblinking at him with huge, terrified eyes. His mouth worked, a low "ahhhh" sound escaping between sagging lips.

"I'm sorry. She shouldn't have left you like this."

Within the beat of a breath, Joseph snapped the man's neck. He then rose and stepped over the corpse to face whatever Dana had left inside.

The smell seared into him, a mélange of human refuse. He walked between bodies, careful to avoid congealing puddles. In all his years of roaming the planet, he couldn't remember seeing death such as this. He'd seen disease, burning, humans crushed, ripped to pieces, impaled, almost anything one being could do to another, but this was new. It appeared something deep inside these men had sought escape, snuffing them out of existence in a pulse of energy.

Four bodies. No Alexander.

Interesting. The man had to have been here. Dana wouldn't have reacted as she had otherwise.

These deaths did not bother him. They no doubt had it coming. What bothered him were the implications. His fledgling was powerful. Too powerful. Dangerous to humans, yes, but possibly dangerous to her own kind. He remembered that electrical current running over his flesh, the hum of it in his head. It had been unpleasant and she hadn't even been aware of it.

Maybe he should have let her die. It might have been for the best.

The thought brought a deep pang of sadness and he closed his eyes for a long moment.

No. These men deserved their endings. If they'd left her be, they wouldn't be drawing maggots. She'd protected herself and someone she cared deeply for. There was no crime and she shouldn't suffer for it. For better or worse, she was his child.

Joseph wheeled around, expecting the generator to the old place might have enough fuel for one hell of a campfire.

****

Alex awoke to the firm insistence of a hangover headache.

Blinking, he brought his surroundings into focus, confused at the familiar scent of the room and the cushions beneath him. Night slunk in from between the living room blinds and one lamp burned to press it back.

Memory slapped him and he sat up too quickly. His brain seemed to vibrate in his skull and he sunk his head into his hands to still it. His thoughts were murky, convoluted, and nausea twisted his stomach.

Dana wasn't here. He knew it before he'd opened his eyes. She'd disappeared to finish what someone else had started.

His stomach took a sudden heave and he stumbled off the couch, dropping to his knees in the tiny bathroom off the front entry just in time. His body was determined to rid itself of every last ounce of sustenance he'd absorbed, in addition to something else that couldn't be so easily purged. Everything came up until empty retches filled the confined space. Dark spots danced before his eyes even as sweat coated him and his muscles trembled.

Alex stayed in a weakened heap between the toilet and the wall, waiting for it—whatever *it* was—to pass. It felt like the fucking flu, but what kind of flu explodes all over you in the space of minutes?

Light flickered in the back of his mind. Dana. She was always there, but this light was purified emotion wrapped in something new. Knowledge? Intuition? Of what? What the hell was this? It wavered inside, like a candle darting deep inside his head. He pressed his fingers to his eyes, took several cleansing breaths, but it remained.

He staggered to his feet to grasp the edge of the sink and gazed at his reflection in the mirrored medicine cabinet.

A death white complexion greeted him, the stubble of his blond beard an unusual sharp contrast. Darkness sunk in around his eyes, making them resemble pained, glassy stones in a deep mine. If he didn't know better, he'd swear he was looking at a stranger hopped up on amphetamines.

The light inside pulsed again, moving, etching a channel. A cry sprung from between his lips and he clutched his head, pressing his temples, massaging to extinguish it.

Need and instinct blended together. His rational

mind tried to bat it away, dismissing it as one would a carnival fortune teller, but a primal, animal part rose to attention, scenting the air, ready to follow his mate.

Mate? What the fuck? Where had that *even* come from?

Alex wanted to scream, wanted to bash his head against the sink, seeking blood, unconsciousness, and peaceful darkness. His muscles clenched and shook, painful in their fervency, eager to dump him to the floor or send him running with mindless intent.

Her light continued to flicker.

Panting, he twisted, stumbled and fell against the wall, pulled himself up, and walked on rubbery legs toward the door. He paused only to sweep his keys off the coffee table where Dana had dropped them.

Chapter Twenty-Five

Patricia Caras lifted her daughter into the back of the car while the airport porter loaded their luggage. Her eight-year-old son climbed in after them, bouncing on the seat before settling in the corner with her phone.

Olivia cuddled against her, bright green eyes glassy with fatigue, thumb poking toward her mouth. Patricia should have stopped her, but the little girl rarely reverted to her infant behavior. It was just a sign that she'd hit a wall and was ready to sleep for the next twelve hours. When they got home, Charles would carry her to her room before making sure C.J. got to bed. Patricia would insist on it. They'd missed their father and deserved a little one on one attention. After which would be her time. She deserved a little tender loving, one on one, too.

She'd brought them back to Seattle ahead of schedule after the children had become restless and homesick. In truth, so had she. Family was lovely to visit, but they wore on her nerves with their constant *suggestions* for how she should raise her children or how to be a better wife. Patricia was ready to scream when her aunt asked whether Charles was satisfied in bed and how she should be careful because men will stray when bored.

Charles could be moody, distant, and abrupt, but also loving and romantic. In her heart, she knew he wouldn't cheat on her, but paranoia planted and now thriving, she'd strolled Rue Saint Honoré in Paris for a few select pieces of lingerie. She planned on modeling them tonight and couldn't wait to see her husband's surprise.

"Straight home?" Roger slid into the driver's seat and turned to peer at her. He'd been in Charles's employment for six years and his long, hang dog face never cracked a smile from what she could remember. However, he was always respectful. Of all the men who worked for her husband, she supposed she liked him best. "Please. The children are tired."

"Am not!" C.J. glowered up from behind the phone.

"Shush." Her nanny had requested to spend some additional time with her parents in Dublin and Patricia already regretted giving her permission. C.J. could sometimes be such a handful. She offered the driver a smile, mildly embarrassed. "Home."

Roger nodded and pulled away from the curb.

****

Victor made several turns through the affluent community, his face blank. The sheen of his forehead and the dank aroma he gave off though his pores were the only indication of the turmoil brewing inside.

She sat across from him, one leg pulled up and under her, watching. This man wasn't the only one with all forms of primal energies pulsing within. While under her influence, he'd told her everything with a soft smile and distant gleam in his eye. Now as they drove toward the man who'd sent her life plummeting into a half-existence, Dana wrestled with the tempestuous blend of rage, sorrow, fatigue, and her own fear of losing herself. The cabin had been something larger than her, something beyond any real control, a defensive reaction resulting in ghastly death. But now she'd gone on the offensive and while her human part steeped in sadness and horror, her vampire-self whispered of retribution.

Nausea seesawed through her belly at the struggle, exacerbated by this man's dark and oily aura.

More than once she considered leaping from the car just to escape his presence. Anger kept her still. She no longer feared this Caras person would come after her. She was more than capable of taking care of herself. What scared the hell out of her was the possibility of him using another of her loved ones to get to her. How could she protect everyone? But, then again, could this man be that arrogant to believe he could control her? Or be that stupid?

Dana frowned, considering. After what had occurred at the cabin, perhaps the very real threat of a grisly death could *dissuade* him from pursuing her or her family. As much as Caras deserved his dark fate, the person she used to be dug in, shaking her head, whispering of humanity.

She studied Victor, watching him squirm under her scrutiny. He'd done horrible things. His deeds pulsed from him, thick and vile. They were ambiguous, but her imagination remained sharp. He couldn't be the person he now was without perpetrating darkness. Another deserving of death. Another who could be controlled by fear. He stank of it. Sociopaths didn't hold any emotion for others, but they sure as hell strove to protect their own asses.

Maybe the night that began in death and horror didn't have to end that way. But she'd have to keep her emotions under control. As long as she didn't lose her temper, she might be okay.

He made a left and they reached a dead end barricaded by a ten foot block wall broken only by an ornately carved gate, wicked spires topping the crest. Tapping a passcode on the keypad at the entrance, he waited several moments before electronic clearance was granted. The circular driveway arched toward an impressive English Tudor with spiraling turrets and

heavy paned windows.
****

Charles Caras sipped his scotch and stared into the flickers and twists of flames alive, yet still imprisoned, within the huge rock fireplace. A semi-automatic handgun lay on the end table just to his right.

He hadn't liked what he'd heard in Victor's voice. It was something he'd never heard in their eight plus years of association. He replayed the conversation over and over, the words turning secondary, leaving panic standing alone. It was hidden well, but Caras could identify it through the shifting timbre of the man's tone.

Not an ordinary vampire.

What the hell did that even mean? What *was* an ordinary vampire? He'd always thought them to be figments of fertile and deranged imaginations. When they were outed years back, he still didn't buy it. The stories were ridiculous. Just tales designed to frighten the weak-minded and Caras was anything but weak-minded.

And now it would seem one of those stories might be coming for him.

Caras finished his drink and set the tumbler next to his weapon.

Just to be cautious, he'd arranged an anonymous tip regarding a rogue vampire. He made sure the old forestry service cabin was mentioned, keeping it vague, but with just enough information to prick a reporter's interest.

When he heard the door and whisper of voices from the front entry, his first thought was one threaded with a surge of warmth inside. Patricia and the children were home. A moment later, unease chased the thought away. It was too early. They weren't due in for another couple of days.

It was probably one of his men checking in. His

house attendant, Allison, must have buzzed open the gate. He almost smiled, a thin chuckle rising to remind him of his foolishness.

But he wasn't an idiot either.

He pushed from his leather club chair, grabbed his handgun and shoved it in the pocket of his cardigan. Striding from the warm tones of his den, he entered the cool elegance of the front entry.

Allison leaned against the door as if her legs didn't want to support her weight, hand clasped on the handle. Victor stood before her, looking beyond the girl, gaze finding and locking on Caras.

Anger and temper merged and Caras pulled his lips back from his teeth in a snarl.

"What the hell are you doing here, Victor? I remember expressly telling you to stay away from me. Or were those instructions too vague for your scared little rabbit brain?" The words might come back to bite him, but at the moment he couldn't care less.

The man didn't immediately answer, but his face looked pale and strained. His deep-set eyes darted away and around the entry before returning to Caras. That's when he thought he saw a twist of terror and rage. "Do you believe in karma, Charles?"

"What are you talking about? What's the matter with you?" Caras stepped forward, faltering as a low heated vibration crept over his skin. He blinked, annoyance disappearing in favor of caution. "What *is* that?"

"I'm sorry. That's probably me." A low and silky voice reached his ears at the same time a young woman stepped from behind Victor, keeping one hand on the man's arm. Her dark eyes sought his, persistent in their endeavor. "I'm still learning to deal with things."

Caras thought he might be falling, but he was

fairly certain his legs were still under him. A warm haze sifted into his brain as he absorbed the beautiful creature before him. Distant bells of warning blared, but her gaze assured him all would be well. Logically he knew that wouldn't be the case, but the thought floated around his periphery. "You must be Ms. Chambers."

"And you're the man who destroyed my life."

He smiled, hoping it was charming, unsure because of the murkiness. "It was nothing personal."

"I'd like to come in."

His smile didn't falter. "The old stories tell me it's unwise to invite a vampire into one's home."

"They're just fables, Mr. Caras." She beamed at him, just a hint of elongated canine sliding through. "I'm just being polite."

Caras stepped back. "Please come in then."
****

Alex followed the flickering in his head.

Her light pulsed inside, beckoning him, somehow warm and disquieting in one incongruous motion.

He had no fucking idea where he was going. He just drove, heading west on the interstate. Brain hazy, he drifted more than once, only to jerk aware with the blast of an irritated horn.

His body burned up, sweat coating his face in a glistening mask, but the compulsion took over. His need stood greater than his common sense.

Winding up on Mercer, he exited the freeway, and continued to take his turns as if he'd grown up on the island instead of the elevated terrain of Issaquah.

He parked the truck a couple blocks away from her. The light in his head had ceased to move, but he could feel her turmoil. Climbing out, he leaned forward and braced his hands on his knees. Alex gulped in cold air, trying to regulate his breathing, failing. Gritty vomit rose in his throat and he swallowed it down, the burn leaving an aftertaste that threatened to bring the sickness full circle yet again. Squeezing his eyes shut, he concentrated, reining it in.

When the urge to throw up passed, he shoved his hands in his pockets, caressing the grip of the .38. He didn't know if he'd need it, but he felt naked and exposed without it. He pressed forward, keeping his head down and staying in the shadows. He wasn't sure of any plan, his logical mind long since muddled. His confusion was white noise, but the razor need and pressing instinct propelled him forward.

A light rain began to fall.

****

The steady push gone, Dana stepped over the threshold. "We have a few things to discuss."

The man continued to smile benignly at her, but she knew the moment she let him go, it would drop away to be replaced by something cold and calculating. She just had to control her emotions to get past her simmering rage. It built in her. That force, that terrible power, flexed and pulled at her thin strand of control.

A pale haze of little blemished aura surrounded the other woman and Dana heard her whimper in terror. After only a moment of indecision, she addressed her. "Go home. You don't belong with these men."

Despite her gentle tone, the woman continued to cry. "I can't."

"Tell her she can go."

Caras smiled and nodded. "It's okay, Allison. You can go for the night."

Without another word, the young woman turned, stumbled, righted herself, and fled into the darkness surrounding the big house.

"I'm not sure if she was more afraid of me or

you." Dana sized up the man before her. He wasn't big, but exuded a carefully maintained power that emanated from his core. Someone used to being in charge, being in control. Someone who pulled strings to make others dance.

The emotional blow inside made her stumble sideways.

What the hell was he doing here? How could he...? Alex's proximity pulsed through her and she swung her head toward the door.

In that moment of distraction, Caras blinked back to himself, and reverted to instinct. He pulled his weapon, shoved it into the vampire's chest and pulled the trigger, noting Victor's growing distance. He backed away and Caras rolled his eyes.

Even as the sound reverberated through the soaring entry, the creature folded to the floor of the shining entry without a sound, blood oozing from the open wound.

And here he'd been told these things were difficult to kill. He shook his head in bemusement.

Ridiculous superstitions.

****

Patricia gently smoothed the slumbering little girl's hair as she watched Roger take all the familiar turns home. Exhaustion nibbled at her, trying to pull larger pieces out, but she knew her second wind would kick in the moment she laid eyes on Charles. He was her elixir.

The driver slowed to access the heavy gate and a moment later, they passed through, the big house welcoming them at the curve of the driveway. Just the sight of it brought a profound warmth of comfort. Home. Finally.

They pulled close to the front door and Roger

immediately hopped out to loop around the back to grab their luggage.

The little girl continued to sleep, but C.J. stirred from the restless doze taken on the way home. Grabbing onto the phone, he sat up, a smile curving his lips, brightening even more as he recognized his surroundings.

Patricia winked at her son and maneuvered to scoop her daughter into her arms. The child's head lolled against her shoulder as she climbed from the vehicle. She sucked in a gasp when she turned to find herself face to face with a man she didn't recognize.

He was handsome with wavy dark blond hair and intense blue eyes, but heavy shadows creased his face. A sheen of sweat coated his skin and the heat of fever rose from him. She took a step back, hugging the girl to her and putting her body between her son and the stranger.

A junkie. Dear God.

The man had appeared like a shadow and she could still hear the driver gathering their things.

"Roger...?"

"Ma'am?" He popped up to gaze at her over the roof of the car, freezing for a moment before reaching into his jacket.

"No, don't do it." The blond man flashed his own handgun and Patricia went cold and still, terror immobilizing every muscle. Stepping forward, he took the driver's weapon and shoved it in his pocket. He glanced over his shoulder, expression pinched. "I'm a cop. Don't approach the house. It's not safe."

"Who *are* you? What are you talking about?"

"Mom?" C.J. turned big eyes between his mother and the stranger.

"Shhh, it's okay." She knew her words carried no weight, but she cleared her throat to tame the waver and tried again. Using a tone she used when dealing with the help, she schooled her face, trying to ignore the man's weapon. "I don't know who you think you are, but I want you to leave right now. My children are tired and need to go to bed. Roger? Can you please call the *real*—"

She cut herself off, frowning as she watched her house manager dart out the front door. The woman paid them no attention and cut across the lawn.

A sharp crack pierced the night and the man before her stumbled as if hit, face paling almost translucent. He caught himself before he could fall.

"Oh, my God. Was that a gunshot?" She stared toward her home, voice rising to strident. "What is going on?!"

"Stay here," the man gasped, backing away.

"Dad!" The boy pushed past them, running for the steps.

"C.J.!" Patricia screamed, her heart pounding hard enough to deafen her, panic rooting her into the ground.

The man twisted around to give chase, following the boy up and into the house.

****

From the corner of his eye, Caras saw movement. Giddy, control wavering, his heightened senses to a truly interesting evening had him swinging around and aiming toward the door. When the unfamiliar man barreled through, he squeezed off another round, only realizing the man hadn't been alone a fraction of a moment too late.

Arctic cold swept through him and Caras froze. His heart stilled in his chest and blood rushed from his head.

The blond man had gone down, but another smaller figure lay tangled beneath him.

His gun hand suddenly leaden, he dropped his arm and stared. Panic and grief rooted him to the tile.

Screaming. All he could hear was screaming. Feminine cries from outside, his own building within his lungs and exploding.

The tow-headed child lay still, partially shielded by the man's body. He thought he saw a splotch of red but couldn't determine who it belonged to. For the longest moment, the tiny figure didn't move. When a wail broke from him, shaking with terror and rage, relief whooshed through Caras. He didn't hear telltale sounds of pain and uttered a soft prayer before stepping forward.

"Dear Lord. C.J.—" A hand from nowhere clutched his throat, cutting off his words and air. A vicious growl sounded in his ears and the next moment he was airborne.

He hit the wall, dully noting the cracking and popping of bones. Something burst within and he bit back a cry when he crumbled against the floor. Caras looked up just as the white face with its blackened eyes rushed him. Her steel grip bunched in his sweater and pulled him close. Her voice trembled as her body did. "You stupid son of a bitch. I wasn't going to kill you. Now, I don't think I can help myself…"

Even as the words left her, a thousand army ants marched over his flesh. The house shook and Caras dimly wondered if they were having the rare Northwest earthquake. Somewhere a window shattered, followed by the loud groan and snap of distressed wood.

She shoved him down and in that moment he realized she didn't have to touch him to bring about his death. Caras began to scream.

In his mind, Victor had escaped to disappear into the blackness of this infernal night, but reality proved so much crueler as he stood watching and feeling the drama unfold before and within him. He became aware of the pulsing of energy around and through him, the buzzing in his head a rash of angry bees. Somewhere he could hear crying, screaming and smell the metallic aroma of blood.

Deep inside, something ancient was determined to escape. He could feel it searching, pressing, looking for weaknesses, cutting through, breaking free. He opened his mouth to scream and managed a gurgle when his own blood built up within his throat.

"Get him out. Hurry."

The harsh words came from the vampire, but they echoed from the other side of the noise in his brain. Victor knew they didn't apply to him. Like ghost images in static, he observed Patricia Caras pull her son into her arms and flee through the open front door. He tried to follow her, but couldn't put one foot in front of the other. His body betrayed him.

Dana Chambers stood deathly still, one hand pressed to her wound, face a study of white nothingness. She swiveled her head his way, the shock of those black eyes rippling through him, but not for long. No, not for long. Agonizing blades cut through his flesh, the house shimmied around them, rare art pieces crashing against the floor, cracks zigzagging through the walls and tile beneath his feet.

Armageddon.

They'd brought this upon themselves.

****

At least the child was safe. She'd managed to control herself enough to keep from harming him or the woman. They were both innocents. Somehow, someway, Charles Caras had kept his darkness from infecting his family.

But Alex was the one who'd sacrificed himself. He'd used his body to protect a little boy who was nothing to him. Grief spiked and she bit down on a wail, a low whimper pushing out instead.

He wasn't dead. The words reverberated through her head.

At least, not yet.

Dana walked toward the prone man lying too still, tears stinging, but not falling. Bullet fragments embedded within slowly worked their way out through muscle, tissue and bone and she gritted her teeth against the agony of healing.

The aroma of Alex's life liquid made her salivate and shame burned through every pore, but she knelt beside him to gently turn him over. Blood coated the side of his face, weeping under her gaze. Eyes closed, they fluttered briefly before a crack of blue appeared.

"Brave and foolish Alex." She rested his head in her lap, aware of the vibration rising and falling with her distress, aware of the distant wail of sirens. Screams within the soaring and once elegant entry had stopped in a ghastly finish and she paid the two dead men no more thought. "Why the hell would you follow me?" She wasn't sure about the "how," but could only figure their connection was born in friendship and love, cemented in rebirth and blood.

"Had to."

Trembling, she tried to keep it from entering her voice. She curled over to press a gentle kiss to his clammy brow.

Beams splintered and snapped above as the big house fell down around them, but Dana brushed his hair back with trailing fingers, debating, wondering if she even had the strength to help him. Anguish blew through her like smoke, settling its acrid pungency deep inside.

"This is all my fault." He stared up at her, beautiful eyes glassy, unfocused.

"It's not. You need to stop taking responsibility for everything."

****

He didn't agree, but it didn't matter.

At the moment, Alex couldn't tell if the roaring and the swaying was in his head or if the house was indeed shaking to pieces. He could still feel her power snaking its electrical essence over him and it seemed to ebb and flow with her sobbing. Pinpricks of fire paraded along his skin and muddy memories from earlier tonight slid into his brain. Was it really just tonight? It just seemed so unbelievable.

Her appearance was all vampire, bone-white and black liquid eyes, but her voice remained Dana with its honey-infused throatiness. He allowed his lids to sink shut and pictured her in the glorious daylight. Glowing skin, beautiful but sad smile, her dark hair simmering in the sun as the wind tossed it around her shoulders. He remembered that low, sexy laugh during their last dinner, how it shifted into a girlish giggle after her only drink of the evening. He thought about their first kiss, how she fit so perfectly in his arms as they'd danced.

No more. He wanted to weep, but didn't have the energy. He was colder than he'd ever been before. Needle-sharp daggers of ice sunk into his flesh and bones and some part of him knew he was going into shock.

Dana leaned over to kiss his lips and held him tightly when the rumbling and sudden darkness turned him deaf and blind.

Chapter Twenty-Six

Samuel Cleary eased into his worn leather recliner with Jasper and Bokken lying on either side. His fat beagle vibrated with gusty snores, while Dana's big mix rested quietly, but awake. The dog remained on alert the entire time he'd been staying with him, echoing Sam's own inner turmoil.

After not hearing from his daughter for several days, his unease had managed to creep inside and bloom into severe anxiety. Seeing her at Alex's condo had done nothing to soften his concern either. He'd felt a little murky, which was odd, but on the drive home, his parental instincts came into full swing. In his gut, he knew something was deathly wrong.

Of course his subsequent calls had gone unreturned.

Sam hated feeling helpless. He'd been forced to stand by and watch his wife waste away from disease when Dana and her brother were children. Now déjà vu prickled across him, an itch he couldn't scratch.

He reached for the remote and clicked on the TV more for noise than anything. His mind was too full of worry induced static to concentrate on anything.

Dana was bumping up against 30 and valued her independence. He understood that and respected it, or at least he tried to. She *was* his baby girl, after all. In honesty, he knew it had almost killed her when she'd been forced to rely on others during her recovery. Even after she'd been discharged, physically she'd been incapable of living alone. She'd returned to live in her childhood home with him, resenting it the whole time. Not vocally. She was too polite and respectful for that.

But the anger and annoyance from being too sedentary, the flare of her temper when she didn't progress as she'd expected, had been a constant source of strife. Sam hadn't envied the poor woman who had come out routinely to work with her one bit. A physical therapist with a soft, southern demeanor and the iron will of a Super Bowl coach had gotten Dana back on her feet, even running, despite the challenge of dealing with a surly patient. The compound fractures in her leg and the broken hip had settled into memory with the exception of a slight limp when she was tired. The head injury was something she continued to deal with and probably would the rest of her life. Sam chose not to ponder that, the fear of losing his youngest child after losing her mother years back, too much to bear.

During all the time she'd spent recovering, Alex Kelly had never been far. He'd come by several times a week to visit, maybe bring her favorite burgers or some teriyaki, sometimes sit out on the dock with her for hours. He'd even take Bokken for a run for her. The man was over the moon in love with his daughter, but kept it close to his chest. Awkward situation, that's for sure. Sam wondered if Dana even knew.

Bokken's sudden loud, deep bark made him jump and he stared down at the animal with a heavy frown. "What's that all about?"

The dog whined and got to his feet to pace the living room before parking himself at the door leading downstairs to the clinic. The whine graduated into the rumble of a growl, waking Jasper who waddled over to see what the fuss was all about.

Both animals lowered their heads, tucked their tails and the cacophony of deep throated barks from the big dog and howls from the beagle filled the living room. Hackles rose, muscles tensed and Sam stared at them, startled. Low level concern curdled inside, but he'd be damned if he'd let it morph into fear. This was his home.

"*No* bark!"

Bokken and Jasper ceased at the command, but continued to whine with the same urgency.

A moment later, the downstairs buzzer sounded, setting off the dogs a second time.

Emergencies weren't all that common, but they did happen. Folks would bring in their suddenly sick cat or perhaps a dog that had been hit by a car, but the fearful energy and vibration filling the room didn't match that scenario. Maybe Jasper was just feeding off Bokken's anxiety, but even Bokken had never acted like this before. He knew the dog well, had even helped raise him.

"No bark."

The riotous sound stopped again and Sam stepped past them to the hall closet to pull the gun lockbox from the top shelf. In seconds, the LCP was out, checked, and in his palm.

"Okay, boys. Let's go see what's what."

He threw open two heavy deadbolts and stepped from his private home into the stairwell leading down to his veterinary practice. From his vantage point, the steps doubled back on themselves, so he couldn't see the frosted glass door with his name etched into it.

Sam absently patted his pocket to verify he hadn't lain his phone down somewhere and crept downstairs, pistol in hand. Both dogs pressed close, suddenly quiet, hackles still up.

He turned at the switchback and the tall counter his receptionist hid behind came up on his left. Just before him, two figures blurred behind the door. They leaned together, the smaller supporting the larger.

What the hell was this?

"Dad?"

Her soft voice reached his ears and breath whooshed from his lungs. Without pause, he flicked the locks open and pushed the door outward. "Dana? What's going on?"

Both dogs broke into a torrent of barking to drown out his words.

"Bokken. Quiet down. You too, Jasper." She didn't raise her voice, but her tone meant business. The beagle backed away, shaking, but Bo dropped to his belly, watching them with troubled eyes.

Sam ignored the animals, instincts bringing him forward to grab hold of the younger man's other arm. Alarm raced through him. Even in the low light, he could see the pallid face and blood. "What the hell happened?"

"He was shot."

"Just a graze..." Alex mumbled.

"He was *shot,* Dad. I need you to help him. Please."

"After all this, she takes me to a dog doctor..."

They both ignored him.

"Jesus, Dana. He should be in a hospital..." he squinted at his daughter, but she kept her head down, hiding her face in the draping of her hair.

"It's not in his best interests. You have to trust me. He'll be okay. I just need you to take care of him. I think he's in mild shock." Her voice shook, closing in on a growl. "I'm sorry. I have to leave."

"Oh, no you don't. Dana Catherine, you're going to help me. You're basically telling me I can't report this, so if I'm taking a risk here, you can at least assist me. I want to know what's going on with you two." Fear churned inside him and he barked orders in response.

"I can't..." she pleaded now and something conflicted tugged inside him. His child was in pain and there was nothing he could do. Except for what she asked.

"Sam, you need to let her go," Alex muttered again, meeting his eyes. They were bright with pain, but insistent. "She *needs* to leave…"

Releasing Alex, Dana backed away. When Bokken slid out the door to follow her, she dropped into a quick crouch and brushed his fur with her fingertips. "You have to stay here and watch over dad and Alex."

The dog whined and showed his belly.

"That's my boy. Stay here."

Sam couldn't tell if it was a trick with his eyes or just a random pair of headlights washing over her face, but in that moment, when her hair fell aside, her skin looked cadaverous. Before he could blink, she was gone.

Chapter Twenty-Seven

Dana somehow managed to reach Maggie's front gate.

She blinked, unsure how it happened. After making sure Alex was safe, she'd spent the last few hours slipping through the shadows. Her brain felt full of sludge, even as her body threatened collapse and her hunger roared. Stray bullet fragments still erupted from her flesh and she'd had to stop several times to close her eyes and bite back the agony.

Now, she stood and gazed up at the decorative waves above the crest of the gate, dimly wondering why she'd felt so compelled to come here. She desperately needed sustenance, but that wasn't it. At least not all of it.

Joseph was here.

Unconsciously, she'd sought him out. On some level the knowledge annoyed her, but twisted deep down within, it brought comfort. If nothing else, he *understood*.

Her muscles refused to budge, choosing to pool instead. She felt like she was falling inside and her legs went watery.

So much anger and fear. So much horror tonight. Daylight beckoned just beyond the subtle lightening to the east. She didn't have a lot of time.

Pinpricks of blackness played behind her eyes, pain and weariness trying to pull her down into premature oblivion.

****

Remorse flickered inside, batting around like the fireflies he remembered from his youth. Joseph tried to swat it away, but the feeling remained persistent, heavy within. With the exception of his rebirth, he didn't remember ever being so torn. It wasn't a natural state for him, so his response was to seek rare distraction within Maggie's arms.

His fledgling had been hurting so much tonight and after dealing with the old cabin, he'd debated seeking her out, ultimately deciding against it. Dana had more than proven she could take care of herself, but the guilt still tormented him.

Maggie sighed softly and he pressed soft lips to her brow. He'd come to her directly from the cabin and they'd indulged in a rare pleasure for the two of them. Killing a woman during lovemaking had once been a real possibility. Not so much now. He'd shed the exuberance of youth many years ago. She'd met him inch for inch, thrust for thrust, passionate and forthright. He'd always admired her fearlessness.

His mind wandered, considering what might be for the best. There'd been some news coverage, but nothing conclusive. It wouldn't matter though. The public were easily spooked like the sheep they were. But humans weren't his primary concern. Years ago, he remembered when their kind had been outed. He also knew what had happened to the unfortunate whistle blower. It hadn't been pleasant.

He didn't want a similar fate to befall his fledgling. She'd done nothing to deserve it, but vampires were wary, suspicious creatures, almost as fearful as their prey. They wouldn't consider the circumstances, only the result.

A moment later, Joseph jolted upward.

"What's the matter?" Maggie pressed the sheet to her breasts and gazed up at him, green eyes sleepy but clearing.

"Dana's here." He leapt from the warm comfort of Maggie's bed, pulling on his trousers before leaving the room, disappearing within a human's limited sight.

The house was eerily quiet, dawn less than an hour away as he descended the stairs, barely touching them in his flight. Panic knotted his insides.

When he burst from the front door, he stopped only for a moment.

She stood beyond the perimeter gate, gazing up toward the peak, as if determining the logistics of leaping over it. Deathly stillness held her in its grip, her face translucent, cheeks cavernous, eyes bleeding darkness.

Joseph had seen starving vampires and if he didn't know better, Dana appeared as if she hadn't fed in weeks.

That infernal power of hers.

Surprised when his anger surged beyond his innate fear, he gritted his teeth. He reached her the moment her legs gave out, scooping her against him. Her head lolled and he could smell blood, tears and dust. He cleared the gate with ease, her weight almost nonexistent.

"Bring her downstairs!" Maggie had thrown a robe on and now motioned him inside. She led him through the entry, beyond the dining room and down a long staircase around the corner from the kitchen. She paused only to pull the door shut behind them.

The stairwell opened into a huge center recreation area, and a hallway split off just beyond the padded bar. "This way."

She pushed through the first door on the right and stepped aside. "I'll get Ty. He's staying over tonight." Maggie slipped away without waiting for a response and Joseph was thankful.

As a father would with a small child, he delicately placed her down upon the four post bed beneath the lace of a high canopy. A low growl pushed from him when he saw blood, but he bit down on it and touched her cheek. "Dana?"

"It's over. It's all over." Her voice, the silk and the sand, was less than a whisper.

"What's over?"

She tried to roll away from him, but he grasped her arm, gentle but firm. "Your assassins?"

"All dead." Dana stared at him long and hard, black eyes unblinking. "Why didn't you tell me he'd be able to sense me?"

Joseph frowned before realization hit and a wave of compassion flowed over him. Alexander. He gentled his voice. "When we feed, we leave ... a trace of ourselves behind. That's why Maggie is sure to rotate her staff. It doesn't always happen, but..." he shrugged.

"You didn't think to warn me?" Her low anger brought out her energy and it slid over the back of his neck, but in her weakness, it dissipated the next moment.

"I'm sorry. I knew it was a possibility, but honestly didn't realize it could happen so quickly." Tenderly, he brushed her hair back from her face, wincing when his fingers touched her freezing skin. "I should have. Is he...?"

Maggie reappeared with a young man and stood aside when he crossed into the room. Without a word, he sat beside the girl's limp form and rested a big hand on her shoulder. "Hey there, gorgeous. You look like you need a little pick-me-up."

Joseph climbed to his feet when the boy stretched out beside Dana, but chose to rest in an adjacent chair to wait.

The young man gathered her to him, exposing his throat, closing his eyes with a tiny smile when she started to feed.

****

Dana curled on her side on the bed, the delicate weave of a handmade throw pulled to her chin and twisted in her fingers. She stared at her maker, fighting the day, but slowly losing. "I've been reported to the media?"

Joseph still reclined in the chair by the wall, having chosen not to leave her side. "A 'rogue vampire' was reported." He curled his lip in disgust at the moniker. "I think it'll be hard for the authorities to connect the cabin with what happened on Mercer, but I can't say the same for our kind. Vampires are very ... *aware* of what goes on around us. We're a paranoid and suspicious lot."

"With good reason, it would seem." She dimly thought of the silver-haired vampire she'd come across that first night. He'd displayed open curiosity before vanishing and she now wondered if he'd sensed her difference.

He lifted and dropped one shoulder. "It's hard to last as long as we have by being careless. I do think it would be best if you left for now. Disappeared long enough to allow everything to settle." Joseph met her eyes. "Perhaps work on some more control."

Nodding, she looked past him to the wall beyond. A Jackson Pollock shared the space, but he doubted she saw it. "Can Alex still sense me? Follow me?"

He regarded her for several moments. "A recent feeding makes it easier, but over time the connection could fade."

"Could? Or will?"

"I think ... often it depends on them." Joseph's eyes turned acute. "Perhaps, how much they love us. They can't always help themselves. Moths battering themselves against a flame or whatever analogy you prefer."

Oh, God. What had she done?

She was so tired, but the ache resonated hollowly inside. Blinking hard, she struggled to stay awake just a few more moments. Dawn beckoned. "Did you make the same mistake once?"

He didn't respond, but sadness fluttered over his handsome features. "You'll be safe here today. Rest well."

And then she was gone.

Chapter Twenty-Eight

The bedroom lamp assaulted his eyes when Alex awoke with the vague aroma of pipe smoke in his nose.

Dana's father perched on the edge of the recliner next to the bed, watching him with intense eyes. A copy of *Field and Stream* was flopped open in his lap and his well-loved pipe lay on the nightstand inches from his left hand.

"Sam."

"Alex."

He squinted at the other man before sweeping the room, thoughts disconnected. His gaze landed on the window, judging early evening from the greying light. Very soon, darkness would come. His heart hitched at the realization.

An uneasy silence had spread through the room and into its corners. He figured the old man waited for some semblance of explanation. Alex wasn't even sure what he could say so he opted for nothing.

"Well, son, seems you've gotten yourself into some kind of fix, cuz you didn't cut yourself shaving there." He waved one hand in the younger man's general direction. "Another inch to your left and you'd be feeding the foliage. Technically, you should be in a real hospital for observation at the very least, yet here you are, hogging my guest bed for almost twelve hours, using my medical supplies, and no doubt eating my food soon. All because my daughter asked me to take care of you before she ... disappeared. Once again, she doesn't answer her phone or return my messages. Since I can't get one from her, I think you owe me some kind of story, don't you? I'd prefer the truth, but I'll give points for a good lie."

A smile pulled at the corner of Alex's mouth, but didn't quite form. How the hell could he tell this man about his daughter? He doubted Dana would even want her dad to know, but it seemed inevitable at this point. He couldn't even fathom a guess to how Sam would react. Everything had tilted onto its side and it was his fault. Despite that fact, Alex didn't regret his actions. Maybe at the beginning he'd wavered, but not now.

With tentative fingers, he traced the bandage above his right eye. The wound throbbed like a toothache and it should have sparked clear memories, but the night before was a thickened haze for him. Dreamlike and indistinct. He tried to concentrate, but his brain wasn't having it, choosing to lunge in pain instead. He just knew it had been one hell of a long night.

Reading his expression, Sam nodded toward the nightstand. A glass of water and a small medication bottle sat next to the pipe. "Best I can do, considering I'm not a human doctor."

Alex nodded his thanks, but made no move toward them. His brain was fuzzy enough without adding narcotics to the mix. He remembered Dana mentioning how her headaches had disappeared. Was that irony or poetry?

"Well, they're there if you need them." Sleep must have been elusive, fatigue wedging deep pockets into the man's face, but for the first time since Dana's accident, blatant fear settled into his eyes, aging his face by another decade. "Look, I know Dana didn't want me to see her last night. She purposely wouldn't look at me and that's not like her. Alex, please, tell me what's happening to my daughter."

Alex shook his head, winced. "Sam, I'm sorry. It's not up to me. I—"

The sun dropped and that tiny light flicked on inside his head, not as bright, but still pervasive, still so damned insistent. He pressed a hand to his head, breath going raspy. Nausea coiled in his belly and sweat popped out all over his flesh.

"Alex? What's wrong?"

Sam's voice became a dim echo from a distant place.

"Feel sick," he gasped it out, rolling off the bed, falling to his knees. He needed to go to her, but he needed to puke first. His stomach rolled as he crawled toward the tiny guest bathroom. Luckily, it was a short crawl.

There was nothing to heave up. He didn't remember the last time he'd even eaten. Yesterday morning? The day before that? His body didn't care and managed to produce a thin string of bile, but the retching motions set off a collision pain in his head, pressing from the inside out, shoving at his wound.

His cry guttural, he fought off the hands grasping him and pulling him up, but was too weak to be successful.

"Alex! Stop it!"

"Got to go."

"What are you talking about? You're not going anywhere."

He pulled away, landed on his right shoulder, stars joining the flicker of light behind his eyes. Grabbing the door jam, he worked to get his feet under him. His legs trembled, but a tiny blast of victory coursed through him.

It was time to leave.

Using the wall for support, he worked his way toward the door, vaguely surprised when Sam appeared before him. Alex reached out to bunch the man's shirt in one hand. "Need to borrow your car."

Sam's brows crunched together, confusion and worry blatant in his eyes. He shook his head. "Not going to happen, kid."

"Shit." Alex slid along the wall, the door just a few feet away. The stairs might be a challenge, but that was okay. He could just go down on his ass. Better than tumbling and breaking his neck. From there, he could call a cab. Or walk. Be a lot easier if Sam would just lend him his fucking car though.

"Alex!" The man bellowed and Alex stared at him, startled, curious.

"What? She's waiting for me. I have to go."

"Listen to me." Sam grabbed his upper arms, strong despite his age. "You were wounded and I promised Dana I'd look after you. You're not in any shape to go anywhere. I need you to lay down and rest." Amusement touched his mouth. "You look like shit."

Alex stared wordlessly for several moments, but he couldn't quite smile. "You're too damned honest, you know that?" He shook his head, pain shooting through it to send him back to his knees when Sam lost his grip. "But you can't understand what's going on."

"No, I can't. You need to explain it to me."

Alex caught his breath, pressing back the nausea and ache. Sweat dripped into his eyes, burning. The flicker of light flared, but this time he managed a smile. "It's okay. She's coming."

****

Dana stopped before her childhood home and took a long moment to soak it in. The big two-story traditional had been renovated 20 some years prior, leaving a generous living area above and an office with space for reception, examination, and treatment below. A separate kennel and cattery had been built just north of the house, parking spread between, deserted on a Sunday evening. Behind the property, the land gently sloped down to a small dock jutting out into the lake. Her father's boat would be tethered there.

She didn't know when she'd see it again. Or even *if* she'd ever see it again.

Her father's aura shifted within and a moment later, his big, burly frame pushed through the glass door, the bell strapped to the handle jingling softly. He regarded her for a solid minute, concern and confusion merging with relief blanketing him. "I can see your face. You're not hiding this time."

"No, Dad."

"Well, get in here already."

He pushed the door wider and she slid past him into the warmth of the front office. The familiar smell of disinfectant and animal food met her senses and she concentrated on it, weeding it away from the aroma of blood pulsing through her father's veins. She'd become all too aware of human vulnerability.

"How's Alex?" She met his eyes briefly before allowing them to flit away.

"He's coming along." He touched her arm, squeezed gently. "Will you tell me what's going on, Dana? Please?"

"I want to, Dad. I do. But I'm not sure how to go about it." She narrowed her eyes against the sting of tears.

"Maybe between you and Alex, you can explain it to me." He turned to climb the stairs and she followed.

When they entered the living room, Bokken greeted her, shrill barks of excitement exiting a wriggling mass of trembling fur. Dana dropped down and gently hugged him, while his tongue sought her ear. The dog knew what she was and didn't care. He loved her just as before.

Just behind him, Alex pushed from the sectional. His pallor matched the white bandage above his brow, but he smiled. His eyes seemed a little hazy, but warmth and unvoiced love settled within. Dana crossed over to him, reached up to caress his check, unmindful of her father watching them. "How are you feeling?"

"Better now. Weirdly enough."

She nodded. "We need to talk, but my dad should know everything first."

"I expected as much."

Dana turned toward where her father stood, uncertainty coating him like ill-fitting clothing. It wasn't something she was used to seeing on him. He'd always been her big, strong, all-knowing dad. Now she realized it was an illusion and it saddened her. "I think you're going to need to sit down."

****

The moon shimmered over the surface of the lake, for once not hiding above overcast skies. Temperatures skimmed just above the freezing mark, but they walked along the shoreline, the air crisp and snapping against their skin.

Her father had taken it better than she would have guessed, but that didn't mean he took it well. There'd been no easy way to tell him, so she'd been blunt, emphasizing it hadn't been a vampire attack. Charles Caras had been the one to indirectly seal her fate. Sam now visited his charges in the kennel to ponder the situation. Even as big of a pill to swallow as it was, like Alex, he preferred her this way to gone forever.

Her own feelings were still a little hazy on the subject.

As they walked, Dana kept an eye on Alex. Her proximity seemed to energize him, or at least quell that compulsion he held inside. They said nothing, but watched Bokken frolic ahead with exuberance, only to loop back to them before repeating the cycle.

She'd gone over everything in her mind to the point of smashing it all into dust. There just were no easy answers. The only thing she could see in the future was vast uncertainty, no matter what choices were made. It was no different from being human. "Alex, I'm sorry for what's happened."

He slanted a look her way. "So, you *meant* to put this thing ... whatever it is ... inside my head?"

"You know what I mean."

"Lots of apologies between us these days." Alex took her hand, rubbing his thumb over her knuckles. "We can't change anything. And holy shit, *a lot* has happened. We can only go forward."

Dana stared down at their entwined hands, gathering herself.

"Is this goodbye, Dana?" Resignation crept into his low voice.

"Only if you want that." She stopped to look up into his face, careful not to connect more than a second or two with his eyes. Maybe it was time for *her* to be a little selfish, but she didn't want to influence him.

Alex tilted his forehead to lightly connect with hers and sighed. "Even if I didn't have this 'link' glowing in my head, I would still follow you to the other side of the planet, if you'd have me." The corner of his mouth pulled into a smirk. "Does that make me co-dependent?"

She closed her eyes, opened them, let them sting and water. "Probably. Or crazy."

"Only crazy if you're going to torture me with country music the rest of my life."

Tilting her head, she frowned at him. "I don't

listen to country music."

"Just making sure that hasn't changed. 40 plus years is a long time."

A laugh burst from her and she shook her head. "You really are crazy."

"I know it."

Dana brushed her fingers down his face, stopped to cradle his cheek. A soft breeze threaded through his hair as pure emotions flooded and overwhelmed her. "I don't know when we might be back."

"I expected as much." He turned his head to press a kiss to her palm.

"I want to bring Bo."

"Okay."

She went on her toes to brush a kiss to his lips. "And I have to leave tonight."

"Tonight?"

"Joseph can't guarantee his kind…" She stopped, cleared her throat. "*My* kind won't come looking for me."

"Do you really think your … talent … could harm another vampire?"

Dana contemplated it. She had no idea, but she did sense a certain wariness in her maker. He wasn't completely sure she couldn't. "I don't know."

"So, it's time to get out of Dodge."

Tears burned and she was reminded of yet another way she was different. There was no world for her any longer. She didn't belong anywhere. Her gaze sought his out for a moment, the sky blue of his eyes connected her to what she once was, what her life had once been. Their beautiful color would continue to evoke memories of perfect summer days and sunlight shimmering against the water. Things she'd never see again.

"You don't have to go, Alex. The compulsion will most likely fade. Your life can go back to normal." Wetness touched her cheeks, and Bokken returned to bump her hip with his big head.

Alex snaked his arms around her waist and kissed her sweet and slow, showing her the depth of his own emotions. "I love you, Dana. I'm sure that's pretty damned obvious at this point. That 'follow you to the other side of the planet' thing? I wasn't even close to kidding."

She swallowed the low sob and kissed him back. His aura enveloped them in a pleasant embrace, familiar and comforting, and she pressed closer.

The ambiguous future waited. It was time to move on. Together.

The End

NANCY E. POLIN

EVERNIGHT PUBLISHING ®

www.evernightpublishing.com

www.ingramcontent.com/pod-product-compliance
Lightning Source LLC
Chambersburg PA
CBHW030256200626
46816CB00002BA/668